The Innocent Imposter

With a superhuman effort, Ursa turned her face away from the Marquis, saying as she did so: "No . . . oh, no! You must not . . . do this . . . please . . . no!"

"Why should we pretend?" the Marquis asked. "I want you, and I think you want me."

"But you . . . must not . . . kiss me," Ursa gasped.

"I cannot think why you should say that," the Marquis argued. There was a touch of cynicism in his voice.

It made Ursa realize that he was thinking of her as Penelope, her sister!

A Camfield Novel of Love
by Barbara Cartland

Camfield Place,
Hatfield
Hertfordshire,
England

Dearest Reader,

Camfield Novels of Love mark a very exciting era of my books with Jove. They have already published nearly two hundred of my titles since they became my first publisher in America, and now all my original paperback romances in the future will be published exclusively by them.

As you already know, Camfield Place in Hertfordshire is my home, which originally existed in 1275, but was rebuilt in 1867 by the grandfather of Beatrix Potter.

It was here in this lovely house, with the best view in the county, that she wrote *The Tale of Peter Rabbit*. Mr. McGregor's garden is exactly as she described it. The door in the wall that the fat little rabbit could not squeeze underneath and the goldfish pool where the white cat sat twitching its tail are still there.

I had Camfield Place blessed when I came here in 1950 and was so happy with my husband until he died, and now with my children and grandchildren, that I know the atmosphere is filled with love and we have all been very lucky.

It is easy here to write of love and I know you will enjoy the Camfield Novels of Love. Their plots are definitely exciting and the covers very romantic. They come to you, like all my books, with love.

Bless you,

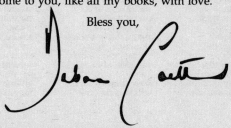

CAMFIELD NOVELS OF LOVE

by Barbara Cartland

A NEW CAMFIELD NOVEL OF LOVE BY

BARBARA CARTLAND

The Innocent Imposter

JOVE BOOKS, NEW YORK

THE INNOCENT IMPOSTER

A Jove Book / published by arrangement with
the author

PRINTING HISTORY
Jove edition / February 1995

ISBN: 0-515-11554-1

A JOVE BOOK®
Jove Books are published by The Berkley Publishing Group,
200 Madison Avenue, New York, New York 10016.
JOVE and the "J" design are trademarks
belonging to Jove Publications, Inc.

PRINTED IN THE UNITED STATES OF AMERICA

10 9 8 7 6 5 4 3 2 1

The Innocent Imposter

Author's Note

THERE is no doubt that when people become blind they often have a perception which is not given to people who are still using their eyes.

This was well known to the ancient Egyptians, who depicted on their statues the Third Eye in the centre of their foreheads.

Amongst the Ancients the eye had always been of tremendous importance.

It was Edgar Allan Poe, the American Poet, who wrote:

"The eyes are the windows of the soul."

This was, however, known right back in the ancient times, when it was believed the eye receives and reflects the intelligence of thought and the warmth of sensibility.

It is the sense of the mind, the tongue of understanding.

The Millionaire businessman who built Port Sunlight, the late Lord Leverhulme, once told me, "To all applicants asking for employment my first attention is given to the eye."

In modern times we have lost the art of using "our third eye" or our perception in knowing whether people are right or wrong, lying or telling the truth.

Hindu sacred legends revered the eye and believed that the Gods could look into a man's soul through the eye.

Josephine de Beauharnais, when Napoleon Bonaparte was trying to marry her, said:

"His searching glance has something singular and inexplicable which imposes even on our Directors. Judge if it may not intimidate a woman."

Napoleon himself agreed with this and said, "I have seldom drawn my sword. I won my battles with my eyes not with my weapons."

Napoleon's eyes were reported to be steady and flickerless even to the end of his very long life.

We are told too that the Indian Emperor Akbar, who achieved the most astonishing success in building up and retaining a very large Empire, had a powerful personality and possessed most distinguished eyes.

The Jesuit missionaries who visited his Court described them as being "vibrant like the sea in sunshine."

What, therefore, could be more powerful than a glance of love between two people when it comes from their hearts.

chapter one

URSA walked in through the front-door.

She thought how quiet the house was now that her Father was away.

She was used to finding him waiting for her in his Study.

Now, instinctively, she went down the corridor as if he were still there.

Matthew Hollington was one of the acknowledged Linguists of the century.

His Library was filled with books written in practically every language in the world.

Some of the books were very old.

He had found them himself in obscure Monasteries, in ancient Castles, even, to his delight, in Oriental Bazaars.

Because Ursa was always with him and he had no son, he had taught her many of the languages.

She had become almost as proficient as he was in knowing if a book or document was genuine or a fake.

1

As she went into the Study she thought again how lonely it seemed when he was not there.

He had gone to Amsterdam for a short visit.

Some scholars there had received documents from the Dutch East Indies which they were finding it hard to decipher without his help and advice.

"Are you taking me with you, Papa?" Ursa had asked.

He shook his head.

"It is not worth it, my Dearest, and you would be terribly bored with the people with whom I am staying. They are all old and obsessed by their own particular interests."

Ursa was disappointed.

At the same time, she knew her Father was thinking of her interest.

Sometimes they had gone on very exciting journeys, but there were others which were incredibly dull.

She had said to him before he went:

"Hurry home, Papa, for I shall miss you. All the same, I have a great deal to do in the garden, and I will exercise your horses as well as mine."

Her Father had laughed.

"I am quite certain you will do that! Take care of yourself, my Dearest, and I promise to be back as quickly as I can."

Because he talked of being away for only a week, Ursa had not thought to ask anyone to come and stay with her in his absence.

She knew that many of her friends would have been glad to do so.

But they talked so much that she would not have

time to do the things she wanted to do.

Hollington Hall was a beautiful Queen Anne house, and Ursa's Mother had made it a real period piece.

It was the delight of many connoisseurs.

She had always insisted that her daughter rather than the servants clean the very valuable china and mend the tapestry chairs.

"If you want a thing done well," she had said to Ursa, "you have to do it yourself."

Ursa knew when her Mother died that that was absolutely true.

She went into the Study.

Upstairs there was some mending to be done in her Mother's room.

The curtains were those originally hung when the house was built.

They were in consequence so precious that it would have been a crime to let anybody less experienced touch them.

She looked around the Study, then tidied her Father's desk.

She lovingly touched the gold ink-pot.

It had been a present from the King of Italy in gratitude for the work her Father had done at the Palace.

"The place was in chaos when I went there," her Father had told her, "but I managed to have everything properly documented, and I only hope they will not mess it up again."

Ursa had not been with him while he was at the Palace, but joined him later.

They had afterwards spent a delightful time in

the South of Italy before they returned to England.

She was wishing she could be with her Father now.

Even if the people were dull, it would be stimulating just to be in Amsterdam.

She hoped he would soon have another more interesting invitation and that she would be able to accompany him.

As she opened the door of the Study, to her surprise she heard voices in the hall.

She wondered who could be calling.

If it was a friend, they would wish to stay for tea.

That, she thought, would prevent her from getting on with the work that was waiting for her upstairs.

She walked down the corridor and met Dawson, the man-servant, who had been with them ever since she had been born.

"Who is it, Dawson?" she asked before he reached her.

"It's Her Ladyship, Miss Ursa," Dawson replied.

Ursa looked at him questioningly.

He realised she did not understand, and said:

"Miss Penelope—Lady Brackley."

"I do not believe it!" Ursa exclaimed.

Her sister Penelope had been married three years before to Lord Brackley.

He was a distinguished Peer who spoke frequently in the House of Lords on Foreign Affairs.

Their Father had met him on one of his trips abroad.

On his return, Lord Brackley had called to see him at Hollington Hall.

He had met Penelope, who was then just nineteen.

He had fallen in love with her, but he had been diffident in his courtship.

He had at first thought that the difference in their ages was too considerable for them to be happy.

This had made Penelope all the keener to marry him.

She had always been extremely bored with her Father's obsession with languages.

She wanted a Social life, which was not available in the country.

Because she insisted, her Father had somewhat reluctantly arranged for her to be presented at Court by a distant Cousin.

He had also allowed her to have a Season in London with the same relative as chaperon.

Penelope had loved every minute of it.

It had made her determined to marry someone of importance.

She wanted to be part of the glittering Social World which centred round the Prince of Wales.

When she came home she talked of nothing but her visit to Marlborough House.

Also the other important houses to which she had been invited.

Unfortunately the Cousin who had chaperoned her did not seem inclined to invite her to stay on longer.

Penelope, therefore, had come back to the country and sulked.

She was bored with everything, even when hunting with a not very impressive pack.

Ursa was perfectly happy as long as she could ride the excellent horses her Father had bought for his daughters.

The friends they had locally seemed to her delightful, and she eagerly accepted their invitations.

Penelope, however, looked down on them and talked of nothing but London.

When Lord Brackley visited her Father he seemed to her like a Knight of Romance come to rescue her.

She sparkled for him, and looked so lovely as she did so.

It was hardly surprising that, although he was over forty, he fell in love.

He had been married before, but the marriage had not been a success, and there were no children.

When he left Hollington Hall he found it impossible to forget Penelope.

He sent an invitation to Matthew Hollington, asking him to his house in London to give his opinion on an old book he had just discovered.

He also invited Penelope.

Matthew Hollington had never envisaged his daughter marrying someone so much older than herself.

He therefore thought it unnecessary for her to accompany him.

Penelope had nearly gone mad at the thought that she might be left behind.

Both her Father and Ursa were astonished at how belligerent she became on the subject.

Of course she got her own way.

After the visit to London, Lord Brackley started to call at the house on one pretext after another.

Finally Penelope won.

He proposed to her in the garden.

She accepted him with an eagerness which was certainly to him very flattering.

Penelope insisted that they should be married in London at St. George's, Hanover Square.

"But you were christened in our Parish Church," Ursa objected, "and everybody in the village will want to see you as a Bride."

"I am not interested in what the villagers want!" Penelope snapped. "Arthur's friends will want to be present at his wedding, and St. George's is the most fashionable Church in London."

Ursa knew there was no point in arguing over the matter, especially as Penelope went on:

"You will be one of my bridesmaids, and as Arthur has a number of female cousins who are all very important, I must have them too."

They went to London before the wedding so that Penelope could buy her trousseau.

Many distinguished people in London had heard of Matthew Hollington and were impressed by his reputation as a gifted Linguist.

But Lord Brackley's friends and those Penelope wished to meet, who all had titles, were interested only in entertaining in the Royal manner.

Penelope walked up the aisle on her Father's arm wearing a glittering tiara that belonged to the Brackley family.

She was followed by ten bridesmaids, all of whom, with the exception of Ursa, had titled parents.

As soon as Penelope and Lord Brackley had left on their honeymoon, Matthew Hollington and Ursa went back to the country.

"It is nice to be home, Papa," Ursa said.

"Do you mean that?" he asked. "Or are you, too, my Dearest, aching for the glittering lights and a husband who wears a coronet?"

He spoke with a twinkle in his eyes, but Ursa replied quietly:

"When I marry, Papa, I want to be in love, as you and Mama were."

Her Father put his arm around her.

"That is what I hope you will find, my Dearest," he said. "Real love is the most wonderful thing in the world."

He kissed the top of his daughter's head and said:

"Because I believe in Fate, I am sure one day you will find the right man, and not end up with second best, however dazzlingly he may glitter."

Ursa knew exactly what he was saying, and she kissed him before she said:

"I am sure you are right, Papa. In the meantime, I am more than happy to be with you."

She knew her Father was pleased by what she said.

She also knew that now they had lost Penelope for good.

She sent them postcards while she was on her honeymoon.

After that she wrote to them at Christmas, sending them useless, inexpensive presents.

Ursa could not help wondering how much she spent on her distinguished friends.

As Lord Brackley was very rich, she was sure it was a considerable sum.

"What am I supposed to do with this?" Matthew Hollington asked.

He had received the following Christmas a penholder which was too small for the type of pen with which he wrote.

"I am sure it will come in useful for the next Bazaar, Papa," Ursa replied.

They both laughed.

Ursa's presents were, she guessed, things that Penelope had received from other people but for which she had no use.

They too were kept for the local Bazaar.

The letter of thanks they received from Penelope for the presents they had sent her was short.

It was obviously written in a hurry.

In fact, as time went on, Penelope became a shadowy figure who did not seem to belong, Ursa felt, to the Hollington family.

She read about her in the Court Circulars.

But it was difficult to think of her as the sister with whom she had shared everything as children.

That included a Nanny and a Governess.

Penelope, however, had never understood anything her Father tried to teach her.

Ursa, on the other hand, found everything he told her enchanting.

Because he had a command of words, he conjured up for her the Palaces of India and the snow-capped mountains of the Himalayas.

He made her see the beauty of Persia and the Pyramids of Egypt.

Now Ursa often went with him on his trips abroad.

By this time, Penelope had gone to Finishing School, where Ursa, when she was old enough, was to join her.

When the time came, however, Ursa had fought against the suggestion and stayed with her Father.

"How could any School teach me in the same way that you do, Papa?" she asked. "You know perfectly well that you teach languages the way they should be taught, which, as you have said so often yourself, is made such a mess of by English teachers."

Her Father had given in.

Then, because he thought that her Spanish was not as good as it should be, he had taken her to Spain.

After that there had been visits to France and Greece.

It was also very exciting when they went to Russia.

Every time they returned home, it seemed to Ursa that she had learned more, not only about the language, but about the people and their country that was very unlike her own.

"It has been a History and a Geography lesson as well as a lovely holiday, Papa!" she had said once.

Her Father had laughed.

"That is what I thought too," he said, "and, my Dearest, how could I have a better companion with whom to enjoy it?"

His voice sounded very sincere.

No-one knew better than Ursa, however, that he missed her Mother unbearably.

Sometimes, when they went to a place where he had been before with his wife, she would see the sadness in his eyes.

She knew then how unhappy he was without her.

"That is love," she told herself many times, "and I can only pray that one day I will be lucky enough to find it."

Now, as she walked into the Drawing-Room, she felt that her sister was a stranger whom she would have to get to know all over again.

Penelope was standing in front of the mantelpiece, admiring her reflection in the mirror.

When Ursa came in, she turned round and her sister realised how much she had changed.

She looked even more beautiful than she had when she lived at home.

But there was something new about her.

Ursa thought it made her very different from the sister she had known and loved for so many years.

"Oh, there you are, Ursa!" Penelope exclaimed. "I was beginning to think I had come to the wrong house!"

"It is a long time since you have been here," Ursa said.

Penelope made an impatient, but at the same time very graceful movement with her hand.

"Now, please do not start reproaching me," she said. "I have not come home before because I have been so busy with innumerable engagements I could not avoid."

"You look beautiful!" Ursa said in all sincerity.

"I am glad you think so," Penelope answered. "I certainly take a great deal of trouble over myself."

She glanced at her sister's hair as she spoke as if she thought it was somewhat untidy, then turned again to look at her reflection in the mirror.

"I am just wondering," she said, "if this shade of green is a little too bright."

She was wearing a hat to match her dress trimmed with feathers.

Ursa thought it was unsuitably elaborate for the country.

However, it certainly became Penelope, who had just a touch of red in her fair hair.

Her gown too was extremely elaborate.

At the neck were two ropes of pearls, and diamond earrings decorated her ears.

A large diamond crescent-shaped brooch was pinned to her bodice.

"You look as if you are just going to a party," Ursa remarked impulsively.

To her surprise, Penelope put out her hand.

"Come and sit down, Ursa," she said. "I want to talk to you, and I need your help."

"My help?" Ursa exclaimed.

It was the last thing she expected her sister to say to her.

She sat down on the sofa, conscious as she did so that her gown, which she had had for some time, looked shabby beside Penelope's.

She noticed that her sister's face was powdered.

There was a touch of colour on her lips that was not completely natural.

"Are you staying here?" Ursa asked when her sister did not speak. "If you would like some tea, I will order it for you."

"I want to talk to you, Ursa," Penelope said.

She glanced past her sister at the door, and said: "I hope you closed the door."

Ursa was surprised.

"I am sure Dawson closed it," she answered.

"I do not want anyone to overhear what I am going to say to you," Penelope said. "Where is Papa?"

"He has gone to Amsterdam," Ursa replied. "He will be away until the end of the week. I know he will be very sorry to have missed you."

"To Amsterdam!" Penelope exclaimed. "That is excellent! If he does not return for a week, that is exactly what I want."

Ursa looked at her in astonishment.

"What ever do you mean? What are you talking about?"

Her sister bent towards her.

"Now, listen, Ursa, this is very, very important, and I know you will help me."

"I will help you if I can," Ursa said, "but I cannot think how."

It amazed her to think that Penelope, with her important friends, her distinguished husband, and her glittering jewels, could want any more than she had already.

Penelope seemed to find what she had to say difficult.

There was a pause before she said:

"I have come to see you, Ursa, because, as I have already said, I need your help, and it is something only you can do for me."

"Of course I will help you, Penelope," Ursa replied, "although it is difficult to think of anything I could give you that you do not already have."

Penelope looked at her.

Then she said unexpectedly:

"We do not look very much alike, but our voices are very similar."

"Are they?" Ursa asked. "I have never thought about it."

"Of course they are," Penelope said sharply. "You must remember that when you used to call to Mama she often asked, 'Is that Penelope or Ursa?'"

Ursa smiled.

"I do remember her saying that."

"And Papa always used to muddle us up if he could not see us," Penelope said.

She spoke as if she were forcing her sister to agree with her.

Ursa waited.

She could not understand why this mattered one way or the other.

"Now, what I have come to tell you," Penelope said, "is that Arthur is going off to see the Sultan of Tangier, who is a very important man."

"How interesting!" Ursa said. "I remember Papa met him once."

"Arthur will not take me with him," her sister said as if she had not spoken, "arguing that I would be confined with the women in the Sultan's Harem and would not be allowed to take part in any of the discussions, which are long-drawn-out."

"That is quite true!" Ursa murmured.

"He has insisted that I go instead to stay with his Mother, the Dowager Lady Brackley!" Penelope said, her voice sharpening.

"Where does she live?" Ursa asked.

"Not very far from here, as it happens," Penelope replied, "but I have no intention of wasting my time shut up with an old woman in the country!"

"Then why did you not stay in London?" Ursa asked in a puzzled voice.

"Because Arthur is jealous!" her sister replied. "He is determined I shall not see . . . someone I want to see while he is away."

Ursa stared at Penelope.

Then she asked:

"Do you mean . . . a man?"

"Of course I mean a man," Penelope said. "He is very charming, and very attractive, and of course much younger than Arthur, who is making a ridiculous fuss about him."

"So that is why you do not want to go and stay with his Mother," Ursa said, trying to make sense of what her sister was saying.

"That is what Arthur wants me to do, but I have no intention of obeying him."

Ursa stared at her sister.

"B-but . . . he is your husband . . . you have to!"

To her surprise, Penelope smiled.

"Not if you will do as I am asking you to."

"What is that? I do not understand."

"Now, listen," Penelope explained. "Arthur's Mother is now, of course, getting old and, as a matter of fact, is almost blind."

She paused and looked to see if her sister was taking in what she was saying.

"Are you . . . suggesting . . . ?" Ursa began.

"If you want to help me," Penelope interrupted, "you will go and stay with the Dowager Lady Brackley, talk to her, and read to her—whatever one does with blind people—until Arthur returns."

Ursa stared at her sister as if she could not believe what she had heard.

"B-but . . . how can I, Penelope? She will know I am not you!"

"Why should she?" Penelope asked. "She has not seen *me* more than once or twice. She stays in the country, while I am always in London and, as I have said, our voices are very alike. If you make yourself pleasant to the old woman, she should be grateful, as things are, for anyone taking trouble over her."

"But . . . surely . . . when your . . . husband returns . . . ?" Ursa began.

"By the time Arthur returns," Penelope said, "I will be back in London, waiting for him. He has promised to let me know exactly when that will be. I will arrange for a groom to ride over to Brackley Park and wait so that you can send me his letter as soon as it arrives to tell me the date of his return."

"You mean . . . I am to . . . open the letter?"

"Oh, do not be so silly, Ursa!" Penelope protested. "If you are pretending to be me, you *will* be me! You will be 'Lady Brackley' to the servants, and how are they to know that you are not me?"

"I am sure I will . . . make mistakes and do . . . something wrong . . . then you will be . . . furious with me?"

"If you do, you will break up my marriage, and I cannot believe you would want that to happen," Penelope said. "As I have told you, Arthur is very jealous of any man, but especially of Vernon."

She stopped and gave a little gasp.

"I ought not to let you know his name, but he is, I assure you, the most alluring, attractive, and handsome man I have ever met in the whole of my life!"

Ursa stared at her sister.

"Are you . . . s-saying, Penelope," she asked slowly, "that you are . . . in l-love with him?"

"Of course I am in love with him!" Penelope declared. "And he is in love with me. We were in despair because we could not be together. Then like a bolt out of the blue came this wonderful opportunity and we can be together while Arthur is away."

Ursa stared at her sister before she said in a low voice:

"But . . . Penelope . . . you are . . . married . . . you c-cannot mean . . . ?"

"Oh, do not be so naïve," her sister interrupted. "I have told you, I love Vernon, and Heaven knows, I have been a good wife to Arthur, although he is a hundred and eighty and almost tumbling into the grave!"

Ursa was shocked, but she thought it would be a mistake to say so.

"Now, all you have to do," Penelope said, "is to go to Brackley Park in my place and just remember that you are now Lady Brackley, who is one of the great Beauties of London."

Now she spoke with a pride in her voice that seemed to ring out.

Ursa gave a little cry.

"How can I be like that, Penelope?" she protested. "Look at me, then look at you!"

"I am not a fool," Penelope answered. "You are going to look exactly like me. I have brought my lady's-maid with me as well as some of my clothes. She will go with you, although, Heaven knows, I shall miss her."

"Your lady's-maid?" Ursa said as if in repeating the words she must sound like a parrot.

Then, as she realised what her sister had said, she asked:

"Do you mean to say that she knows what you are planning?"

"My Dear Ursa, do stop behaving like a 'Country Bumpkin.' Of course one has love-affairs in London. One has to have someone to open and shut doors, who keeps quiet and who is wholeheartedly devoted to one as Marie is to me."

Ursa could find nothing more to say.

She could only look at her sister helplessly.

She thought it was the most absurd proposition she had ever listened to.

At the same time, she was well aware that Penelope always got what she wanted.

Somehow, although she could not think how, she would have to do what she was told.

As if she knew she had won the battle, Penelope said:

"Marie is waiting in the carriage. I am now going to tell her to go upstairs and help you change your clothes. We will then start on the journey to Brackley Park."

"I cannot . . . I cannot do it!" Ursa wanted to say.

But as her sister rose resolutely to her feet, she knew that any protest she might make would fall on deaf ears.

However frightening the idea might be, she had agreed to impersonate Penelope.

chapter two

URSA stared at herself in the mirror.

She found it hard to believe that she was looking at her own reflection.

Penelope had taken her upstairs to where, to her surprise, her French lady's-maid, Marie, was waiting.

She had already unpacked some clothes that were lying on the bed.

She also looked, Ursa thought, exactly as a French maid should.

"Now Marie is going to make you look more like me," Penelope said, "and you will be surprised how different you soon will be from how you look *now*."

She spoke in a scathing manner which made Ursa feel uncomfortable.

Marie helped her off with her gown and sat her down at the dressing-table to arrange her hair.

She did it in a style, Penelope assured her, that was the very latest fashion.

It made her look older, more sophisticated, and, she admitted, also more attractive.

She said nothing as Marie powdered her face and added a touch of rouge to her cheeks.

Ursa thought her Father would not have approved, but it was no use protesting.

Penelope was telling her what she should know about her life in London.

"We have a large house in Grosvenor Square," she said, "and because Arthur has given over Brackley Park to his Mother, we have a country house near Windsor."

She paused for a moment before she added:

"It is very convenient for Arthur when he has to see so much of the Queen."

Ursa knew she was meant to be impressed, and she said:

"Does he not miss the house in which he was brought up?"

"No, it is too far from London," Penelope answered, "and as his Mother is happy there, he thought it would be a mistake to move her into the Dower House, which is small and ugly."

Ursa said nothing, and after a moment Penelope said:

"To be honest, I have no wish to bury myself in this part of the country. I had quite enough of it when I was a girl, and I remember how dull it was."

"Oh, Penelope," Ursa protested, "we were very happy, you know we were! And when Mama was alive, we used to have the most amusing children's parties."

"You may have been amused by them," Penelope said, "but you are younger than me. I soon grew bored with those dull youths."

She glanced at herself in the mirror and added:

"It was very different when I went to London and found that practically every man in the Social World wanted to dance with me. They paid me compliments, and, of course, they wanted to kiss me."

"But of course you did not let them!" Ursa said quickly.

Penelope did not answer, and Ursa exclaimed:

"You did! Oh, Penelope, Mama would have been horrified if she had known."

"That is only because she lived here in the country, where everybody is prudish and ultra-respectable," Penelope retorted. "Now things have changed, and, I can assure you, Ursa, there are a great number of young men longing for my favours—and one in particular!"

She said the last words in a soft voice.

Ursa knew she was referring to the man she was going to meet.

It was he who was responsible for this extraordinary charade in which she had to play a leading part.

She thought also that it was very indiscreet of Penelope to speak in such a way in front of her lady's-maid.

Marie finished by putting lip-salve on her lips and, to Ursa's astonishment, some mascara on her eye-lashes.

It made her eyes look enormous.

She also realised for the first time that Penelope's eye-lashes were much darker than her hair.

"Now the gown!" Penelope said sharply. "And we have to hurry if we are to reach Brackley Park by tea-time."

"Surely you are not coming with me?" Ursa asked.

"Of course not," Penelope snapped. "Do not be so foolish!"

Because Penelope obviously did not intend to say any more, Ursa remained silent.

She let Marie help her into an elegant gown which was very much like the one her sister was wearing.

It was pale blue with a short jacket in a deeper shade.

"Oh, Penelope, how lovely!" Ursa exclaimed. "Are you sure you can spare this beautiful gown?"

"To be truthful, it is one I do not wear, as I do not like myself in blue," Penelope answered. "It cost a great deal of money, however, as did the other gowns I have brought you."

"I will be very careful with them," Ursa promised.

"I have finished with them," Penelope replied, "so they will be sent to a Charity where I usually send the things I no longer want. I can assure you, the Nuns are always extremely grateful."

"I am sure they are," Ursa murmured.

She could not help thinking that it was just like Penelope not to part with anything she valued personally.

Marie placed an extremely attractive hat on her head that matched the gown.

It was trimmed with what Ursa realised were expensive silk flowers.

"I have given you three other hats," Penelope said, "and Marie will tell you on which occasions to wear them, just as she knows exactly what you should put on for dinner."

She gave a little laugh without any humour in it as she went on:

"I expect you will dine alone with my mother-in-law, and I am sorry for you. But you will have to tell yourself you are doing a kindly act to help me, for which I am extremely grateful!"

Marie produced a pair of expensive shoes with high heels.

Then she gave Ursa a hand-bag and a pair of gloves.

"You are ready at last!" Penelope said. "We must leave at once. It will take us at least an hour and a half to get to Brackley Park."

Marie packed the cosmetics into a small box.

It was then that Penelope gave a scream.

"I have forgotten!" she cried. "For goodness' sake, Marie, how could you let me forget?"

"What have you forgotten?" Ursa asked.

"A wedding-ring!" Penelope answered. "You are supposed to be a married woman!"

She turned to her maid.

"Really, Marie, it is too careless of you!"

Marie murmured, "*À qui la faute?*" Which Ursa knew meant "Whose fault is that?"

She then opened a leather jewel-case.

Penelope searched in it, saying as she did so:

"You are also supposed to be a rich woman.

Of course I cannot lend you anything very valuable, but here are some earrings which I never wear, as they are not spectacular enough, and here is your wedding-ring and a diamond-ring to go with it."

"I hope I do not lose anything," Ursa murmured.

"Oh, they are not the best stones!" Penelope replied casually. "In fact, the diamond-ring was given to me by one of Arthur's relations who, although she is very rich, is also very mean. Otherwise she would have spent more on it!"

Ursa put the rings on the third finger of her left hand.

Penelope went on:

"I have also brought a small diamond star which was given to me by Arthur's Mother. So you may tell her you are wearing it, which will please her. It would be a mistake to lose that, as Arthur would be upset. But he has given me so many magnificent jewels because I insisted on it, that I never wear the star, or the rather small pearl necklace which you can wear in the evening."

"I will be very careful," Ursa promised, "but I have, as you know, some of Mama's jewellery which I can wear if you want me to."

"As my mother-in-law can barely see, it will only be a waste of time," Penelope answered, "and anyway, I am sure they are locked away in the safe and it would take time to get them out."

She spoke sharply and looked at the clock as she spoke.

Ursa picked up her bag.

As they went down the stairs the footman came

hurrying along the corridor to collect the trunk.

As they reached the hall Ursa said:

"I must tell the servants that I am going away, otherwise they will be wondering what has become of me."

"I will tell Dawson," Penelope said, "and I think it would be a mistake for his wife, or those chattering creatures in the Kitchen, to see you."

"Yes . . . of course . . . I had not thought . . . of that," Ursa said quickly.

She had for the moment forgotten that she had been transformed into an imitation of her sister.

"Get into the carriage quickly!" Penelope ordered. "I will talk to Dawson. He too is getting old and blind, and I doubt that, being a man, he will notice any particular difference in you."

She spoke in a low voice.

Then, as Dawson, aware that they had come downstairs, came into the hall, Penelope went up to him.

"It has been delightful to see you again, Dawson! Do tell Mrs. Dawson I am so sorry I am in a hurry and have not time to come into the Kitchen and talk to her. But I am taking Miss Ursa away with me for a few days, which I am sure will make a pleasant change for her."

"T'will indeed, M'Lady," Dawson said, "an' Miss Ursa finds it dull with th' Master away."

"I know she does," Penelope said. "Anyway, look after everything as you always have, and Miss Ursa will be back before my Father returns."

She swept out through the front-door as she spoke.

She climbed into the closed carriage, where Ursa was already sitting.

A footman dressed in the Brackley livery and wearing a cockaded hat shut the door.

As soon as he had jumped up beside the coachman they drove off.

As they passed down the drive and out into the road which led through the village, Ursa said:

"I can hardly . . . believe this is . . . happening. Oh, Penelope, I am so afraid I shall let . . . you down! Supposing your mother-in-law is . . . suspicious?"

"I have already told you that she is as blind as a bat," Penelope replied, "and I was calculating on my way here that she has seen me only four times in her life."

Ursa looked at her sister in astonishment.

"Is that . . . really true?"

"Of course it is," Penelope answered. "She did not come to the wedding because, being blind, she does not like travelling to London, or anywhere else, for that matter."

She spoke scathingly and went on:

"Arthur and I went once to Brackley Park before we were married, and I drove over once with Papa when you were still at School. Since then I have been there twice, when Arthur insisted on my accompanying him."

Ursa did not speak, and her sister continued:

"I can assure you, it was deadly dull, and I was thankful to get away."

"Suppose," Ursa said hesitatingly, "she asks me questions I cannot answer?"

"Oh, just improvise," Penelope retorted. "You are supposed to be the clever one of the family! It cannot be past your capability to answer the questions of a blind woman."

"I . . . I will do my . . . best," Ursa said humbly, "but you must not be . . . angry with me, Penelope, if I make a . . . mess of it."

"I shall be very angry!" Penelope retorted. "But really the only thing that matters is that Arthur should think I am safely ensconced with his boring old Mother! There will be no reason for him to imagine I am—elsewhere."

"And when he . . . returns?" Ursa asked.

"I shall be waiting for him in London with my arms outstretched, telling him how much I have missed him!" Penelope answered. "The most important thing you will learn as you grow older is that men believe what they want to believe, and most of them are so conceited that they cannot believe you do not love them as much as they love you!"

They drove a little way in silence, then Ursa said:

"I always . . . hoped, Penelope, that you would be very . . . happy when you . . . married."

"I *am* happy," Penelope said positively. "It is just a pity that I did not meet Vernon three years ago."

There was a yearning in her voice, and then she laughed.

"Not that he would have looked at me then, if we had met! He has no use for *débutantes*, even though they pursue him madly."

"Then you do not . . . think he would . . . have married . . . you?" Ursa asked.

" 'Pigs might fly,' " Penelope replied. "Men in London, and Vernon is very much a 'Man-about-Town,' like women to be sophisticated, amusing, and, of course, beautiful."

As she spoke, she turned to look at her sister.

"When I see the difference in you, I cannot imagine how you can sit in the country amongst the turnips, and not insist upon Papa taking you to London."

Ursa could not help thinking that if Penelope thought she should go to London, she might have invited her to come and stay with her.

But she only replied quietly:

"I am very happy to be with Papa. You know how interested I am in his work, and I find it fascinating when he is sent, or finds, ancient documents to add to his Library."

"I have always thought it all extremely dull and stuffy," Penelope sighed, "but then, as you know, I was never any good at foreign languages."

Ursa knew this was true.

Penelope had found it extremely difficult to acquire even a smattering of French.

They drove on.

When Ursa thought they must be nearing the end of their journey, she said quickly:

"I am sure there are more things you should have told me about your mother-in-law. Who was she before she married?"

"Oh, no-one of any particular importance," Penelope replied. "Arthur says she was exceedingly pretty, which is why she attracted his Father. But I have no time to ask a lot of questions about someone I never see."

As she finished speaking, Penelope bent forward to add:

"Here we are, at last!"

Ursa looked surprised.

She found they were outside a large Posting-Inn and not, as she had expected, at Brackley Park.

She was about to ask the question, when Penelope said:

"This is where I leave you. Now, remember, from this moment on you are me—not yourself. And for Heaven's sake, suck up to the old woman so that she tells Arthur how charming I have been to her."

The carriage had come to a standstill and the footman was opening the door.

Without saying any more, Penelope got out and hurried through the main door of the Posting-Inn.

Marie, who had been sitting on the box squeezed between the coachman and the footman, climbed down.

She got into the carriage to sit on the narrow seat with her back to the horses.

The footman shut the door and the horses moved off.

It all happened very quickly.

As they drove away, Ursa thought Penelope might have prepared her for what had happened.

She should have told her that Vernon, whoever he was, would be waiting for her at the Posting-Inn.

She thought now that she had seen a magnificent-looking carriage, drawn by four horses, in the court-yard.

It was only a passing glimpse, but she felt it must have been waiting for her sister.

Now that she was alone with Marie, she talked to her in French and the maid was delighted.

"You speak my language like a Parisian, *M'mselle*," she said. "How can you be so fluent, when Her Ladyship is—*mon Dieu!*—so bad?"

"My Father was very insistent that I should speak a number of languages," Ursa explained, "so that I could help him with his work."

Marie then talked about her home and the glamour of Paris.

As she chatted on, it struck Ursa that she was homesick.

She was living in a house where nobody spoke her language and she found it very lonely.

Ursa drew her out.

When she had heard all about Marie's family, she asked about her life in London.

"I come to London," Marie explained, "because Her Ladyship give me very good money, but I miss my home, and of course the man to whom I am engaged."

"You are engaged to be married?" Ursa exclaimed. "But surely it is very sad for you to be so far away from him?"

"We both work hard and save, *M'mselle*," Marie said. "When I go back to France, I have large dowry, and Jacques is also saving so we have leetle house in Paris, and everything we want."

It sounded an ideal aim, and Ursa was interested.

They were still talking about Marie's future when they turned in at the gates of a drive.

"We are here," Ursa exclaimed. "Oh, Marie, help me not to make any mistakes. Her Ladyship will be very angry if I am exposed as an imposter."

Marie laughed.

"You are quite safe, *M'mselle*," she said. "You look now very like Her Ladyship, and in your own way *très, très belle!*"

Ursa smiled.

"Thank you, Marie, and you must keep me looking *très, très belle* until I can go home."

"I will do that, *My Lady!*" she promised.

She emphasised the last two words.

Ursa knew that from this moment she must not only look like her sister, but also think like her.

*   *   *

Brackley Park was an early Victorian house and, Ursa thought, not particularly attractive.

It was, however, impressively large and solidly built.

The garden, she saw, was pleasantly laid out and well tended.

The carriage drew up with a flourish outside the front-door.

A footman ran down the steps, on which there was a red carpet.

He opened the carriage door and Ursa stepped out.

Feeling shy, she walked into the hall, where she was received by a Butler with white hair.

"Welcome, M'Lady," he said politely. "Her Ladyship's looking forward to your arrival and is in the Drawing-Room."

He went ahead to lead the way, and Ursa followed him.

She thought the hall was somewhat austere and lacked charm.

The Butler opened a door and announced.

"Her Ladyship, M'Lady!"

Feeling as if a dozen butterflies were fluttering in her breast, Ursa went inside.

Sitting in a chair by the fireplace at the far end of the room was a woman with white hair.

As she drew nearer to her, Ursa realised that she was still beautiful and had a kind expression.

She was dressed in black, with five rows of pearls at her neck.

The hand that was held out towards hers glittered with several diamond rings.

"Penelope, my dear," she said in a soft voice, "it is delightful to have you here. I was so pleased when I received Arthur's letter."

Ursa bent and, taking the Dowager's hand, kissed her cheek.

"He has gone to Tangier," she said. "He wanted me to stay with you while he is away."

"That is what he said in his letter," the Dowager answered. "As you can imagine, I am delighted to have you with me, although I am afraid you will miss the gaiety that you enjoy in London."

"It is nice to have a change," Ursa said.

"Do sit down, dear child," the Dowager suggested. "Johnson will be bringing us some tea, and I am sure you need it after that long drive."

"That would be delightful," Ursa said.

Looking at the Dowager, she realised that she was in fact completely blind.

It reassured her that she was in no danger of being denounced on sight as an imposter.

She managed to talk about how much she had enjoyed the drive and the countryside, until the Butler and two footmen came in with the tea.

"I am afraid you will have to pour out for me," the Dowager said when Johnson said it was ready.

"Yes, of course," Ursa agreed, "and you must tell me if you take milk and sugar."

She handed the cup, when she had filled it, to the Dowager, and asked what she would like to eat.

"I am not hungry," Lady Brackley replied, "but I am sure you must be, unless, of course, like so many other ladies to-day, you are worrying about having a tiny waist."

"Mine has never been very large," Ursa replied.

The Dowager laughed.

"I remember Arthur telling me, when he described you to me, that your waist was so small that he could encompass it with his two hands!"

Ursa did not know what to say to this, and she was silent.

The Dowager went on.

"You have made my son very happy, my dear. When he told me he was going to marry you, I was worried about the difference in your ages."

She paused as if she were calculating, then said:

"After all, Arthur is now forty-five and I thought he would have been happier with an older woman, but I was mistaken."

"I am . . . glad I have made him . . . happy," Ursa murmured.

She could not help thinking that it was wrong to deceive this charming old lady.

But there was nothing she could do about it now, and the Dowager continued:

"I have prayed that you and Arthur would have a son, but of course you are still very young, and I am sure that God will be kind and send you a baby soon."

"I . . . I am sure . . . your prayers will . . . be heard," Ursa stammered.

"If I am making you feel embarrassed, you must forgive me," the Dowager said. "But I am so much alone that when I do talk to people I tend to express the feelings that perhaps I should keep to myself."

"I hope you can say anything you want to say to me," Ursa replied, "and while I am here, you must allow me to read to you."

The Dowager raised her eye-brows.

"I remember when you stayed here a year ago," she answered, "you told me you hated reading aloud."

Ursa realised she had made a mistake, and she said quickly:

"I expect that was because I felt nervous in case I disappointed you. But this time, I would love to read you anything you would like me to."

She thought how often she had read aloud to her Father.

She also thought it was very selfish of Penelope not to have read to her mother-in-law when she was blind.

"You must go to the Library and choose a book which you think will interest us both," the Dowager suggested. "I am afraid there are not many up-to-date novels, but I am sure you will find something we can both enjoy."

"I am sure I shall," Ursa said, "and to-morrow we will start enjoying, perhaps, a visit to some other country."

The Dowager laughed.

"That sounds delightful. And now, if you have finished your tea, I am sure you would like to go upstairs and rest a little before dinner. It is something I always do, and I expect you are tired after your long journey."

"Y-yes . . . of course," Ursa agreed, remembering that Penelope was supposed to have come all the way from London.

The Dowager rang a little gold bell which stood beside her chair.

The door was opened almost immediately by Johnson.

"Take Her Ladyship upstairs, Johnson," she said, "and ask Martha to come and take me up so that I can rest before dinner."

"Martha's here, M'Lady," Johnson replied.

An elderly maid came into the room and walked towards the Dowager's chair.

"We are both going to lie down, Martha," the Dowager said.

She turned her head in the direction of Ursa and said:

"Penelope dear, you remember Martha? She has been with me for thirty years, and I could not do without her."

Ursa held out her hand.

As she did so, she was afraid that Martha might exclaim that she was not His Lordship's wife.

But Martha only dropped a small curtsy as she said:

"It's been a long time, M'Lady. I thought you'd forgotten us."

"No, of course not," Ursa said quickly. "It is just that His Lordship is so busy that we have not had a chance to get away from London or Windsor."

"Arthur told me in his last letter how much the Queen relies on him," the Dowager said with pride.

Martha helped her out of her chair and was now guiding her across the room towards the door.

"That is true," Ursa agreed, "and he is always being asked to Windsor Castle."

"I only wish I could see him more often," the Dowager said wistfully, "but I must not be selfish, when he is doing so much for the country."

Following them up the stairs, Ursa thought she had taken two jumps without falling.

First Johnson might have realised she was not Penelope, and now Martha.

However, she was quite certain now they had no suspicion.

As she followed her sister's mother-in-law along the corridor, she felt a feeling of relief.

She realised that when she arrived she had in fact been very frightened.

'Now everything is all right,' she thought, 'and I will just make this dear old lady happy while I am here. It must never enter her head that Penelope is behaving in such an improper manner.'

Because she did not wish to criticise her sister, she tried to thrust the thought away.

Yet at the back of her mind she knew that however hard she tried, her sister's infidelity to her husband shocked her.

chapter three

MARIE took a great deal of trouble in arranging
Ursa's hair and putting cosmetics on her face.

"It is very kind of you," Ursa said, "and it is a
pity that no-one can see me."

She gave a little laugh as she spoke.

Marie replied seriously in French:

"There are always the servants, M'Lady, and
they talk!"

Ursa knew this was true.

In a very different tone she asked anxiously:

"Do many of the servants here . . . know my sister . . . by sight?"

Marie nodded.

"*Oui*, M'Lady, but the Housekeeper said how
young you were looking, and even more beautiful
than when she last saw you!"

Ursa had a little throb of fear in case the Housekeeper was suspicious.

"Do not worry, M'Lady," Marie said, "everything's all right, and they are not very clever."

She spoke scathingly, and Ursa could not help smiling.

Parisians always thought themselves clever and quicker-brained than people from other parts of the world, and even from any other part of France.

Ursa was quite sure she would show off her intelligence to the other staff.

When her hair was finished, Marie went to the wardrobe.

"Not the best gown to-night, I think, M'Lady," she said, "but very smart, and you must remember that you are '*La Belle de Londres*.' "

Ursa laughed.

"I wish that were true! But of course when I read the newspapers, I find my sister is always described as being 'splendidly gowned.' "

"I see to that," Marie said proudly.

Ursa thanked her and went slowly down the stairs.

The Dowager liked to dine early, and the sun was still shining outside.

Ursa's skirts rustled silkily as she moved.

The sunlight glittered on her diamond earrings, and she thought she might be acting in a Play.

Then she gave a little shiver.

"At least it is not a Tragedy!" she said to herself.

As she entered the Drawing-Room, it was to find that the Dowager was already there.

As Ursa joined her, she said:

"I have been thinking, Penelope dear, of what book we should read, and I want one which will interest you as much as it interests me."

"I think I am interested in every part of the world," Ursa replied.

Only just in time did she stop herself from saying that she had travelled a great deal.

She had no idea whether or not Penelope had been abroad since her honeymoon.

If she had, it would very likely have been no further than to Paris.

She would have found that City even gayer than London.

Penelope would certainly not have gone to any of the strange places to which she had travelled with her Father.

They had often been very primitive.

The Dowager was following her own train of thought.

"Naturally, I am particularly interested in Greece," she said, "but you may find that rather dull."

"Oh, no, indeed, Ma'am, I am fascinated by Greece," Ursa replied. "But why does it interest you?"

The Dowager smiled.

"Surely Arthur has told you that I have Greek blood in my veins?"

"Of course, I remember now," Ursa replied apologetically, "but do tell me how."

"My mother was half Greek," the Dowager began, "for her Father, who was, of course, my Grandfather, came from the ancient and well-known Greek family of Damacios."

"How interesting!" Ursa exclaimed. "Then, of course, we must read a book about Greece, and especially Delphi, which has always fascinated me."

As she finished speaking, the door opened and Johnson came in to announce:

"Dinner is served, M'Lady."

He crossed the room to help the Dowager to her feet.

Holding onto his arm, the Dowager walked slowly down the corridor with Ursa following them.

When they sat down to dinner, she saw that Johnson cut up the Dowager's food for her.

She ate most of it with a spoon.

She did so, however, very tidily, and Ursa thought it clever of her not to make a mess in any way.

The food was excellent, but very English.

Ursa wondered what her hostess would think if she described the strange food she had eaten when she had been in foreign countries with her Father.

Then she remembered that someone had once told her that if you had to disguise yourself, you not only had to look and speak but to think like whoever you were pretending to be.

"I must think like Penelope," she told herself.

Then she almost laughed aloud.

The Dowager obviously enjoyed having somebody to talk to instead of being alone.

She told Ursa stories of her son Arthur when he was a little boy.

She also said that his Father had insisted upon his being well-educated.

"My husband, if he were alive," she said, "would have been so delighted that Arthur has become such an expert on Foreign Affairs."

"It means, of course, that he has to go abroad quite often," Ursa replied, hoping that was the truth.

"But not as often as he used to," the Dowager replied. "I do feel sorry for you, Penelope dear, thinking of you being left alone in London when Arthur is travelling about Europe."

Ursa could not help thinking that her sister was not alone!

Then she told herself she was being censorious, and there was also a possibility that the Dowager could read her thoughts.

She therefore told her of things Penelope had done when she was a child.

She described their house and the garden.

"I love flowers," the Dowager said. "The one consolation in not being able to see them is that I can still smell their fragrance."

"I have always been told that people who are blind have, through their other senses, a more acute appreciation of other things—like music," Ursa said, "and of course the scent of flowers."

"I think that is true," the Dowager agreed.

Dinner did not take very long, as there were only three courses.

Then Johnson escorted the Dowager back to the Drawing-Room.

When he had left, Ursa said:

"Shall I go now to the Library for a book, or shall we wait until to-morrow?"

"I am enjoying so much just talking to you,

Penelope dear," the Dowager said, "that I think we will wait until to-morrow."

As she spoke, the Drawing-Room door opened and Johnson announced:

"The Marquis of Charnwood, M'Lady."

Ursa looked round in surprise, and the Dowager gave a delighted cry.

As she did so, a tall, handsome young man came hurrying into the room.

"Good-evening, Grandmama," he said, "I am sure you are surprised to see me."

The Dowager held out both her hands.

"Guy, is it really you? I can hardly believe it!"

The Marquis took her hands in his and bent to kiss her cheek.

"It is really me!" he said. "I got back to England three days ago."

"I was beginning to think that I would never see you again," the Dowager said, "and it is very exciting that you are here."

"Hale and hearty!" the Marquis replied. "At the same time, I am in trouble, Grandmama!"

"Trouble? Oh, Guy, what has happened now?" the Dowager exclaimed.

Then, as if she suddenly remembered they were not alone, she said:

"You know Penelope—Arthur's wife—of course!"

As she spoke, Ursa drew in her breath.

It flashed through her mind that she was about to be exposed.

The Marquis, however, held out his hand and said:

"No, Grandmama. In fact, we have never met.

I was abroad when they were married and have been ever since, or in the country."

He paused and smiled at Ursa, then continued:

"But of course I have heard a great deal about the beautiful Lady Brackley."

"You have never met each other?" the Dowager queried in surprise. "Then it is very fortunate that she is here to keep me company, because Arthur has gone to Tangier."

The Marquis smiled.

"I am delighted to make your acquaintance, Penelope, if I may now so call you?" he said to Ursa. "I met a friend of yours a few months ago who was ecstatic over how lovely you were. Now I see he was not mistaken!"

Ursa hoped she would not blush, as she was sure Penelope would not have done.

But she felt shy because she was not used to compliments.

Nor, she thought, on all her travels had she ever met a man as handsome as the Marquis.

"You say you are in trouble, Guy?" the Dowager asked questioningly.

"I am in deep trouble, Grandmama," the Marquis said, "and that is why I have rushed here from Charnwood, to beg you to help me."

He pulled up an armchair beside her and sat down.

As he did so, Johnson came in with a bottle of champagne on a silver tray which he set down on a small table next to the Marquis.

"Pour me out a glass, Johnson," the Marquis said. "At the speed I have been travelling, I need it."

"Your Lordship's coachman has taken the 'orses to the stable, M'Lord," Johnson replied, "and I understand Your Lordship is to stay the night?"

"I would like to, if you will have me, Grandmama," the Marquis said to the Dowager. "I do not particularly want to drive home in the dark."

"No, of course you must not do that," the Dowager agreed, "and you know how delighted I am to have you."

Johnson poured out the champagne, then left the room.

The Marquis sipped a little before he said:

"Now I will tell you why I have come."

Ursa looked at him and said:

"Perhaps you would prefer to be alone with your Grandmother. In which case, I will retire."

"No, no, not at all," the Marquis quickly replied. "You are part of the family, and it is, I assure you, very much a family problem."

Ursa had half-risen from her seat, and she sank down again.

The Marquis put his hand into the inside pocket of his coat and drew out a letter.

He glanced at it, then put it down on his knee and began:

"As you know, Grandmama, I went out to India at the invitation of the Viceroy. He entertained me royally, and I enjoyed myself enormously. While I was in Calcutta, I was shown over two of our Battleships there and found they lacked the latest armament and improved equipment."

He paused and then continued:

"I mean such as is designed for the Battleships that are being built at the moment in this country."

The Dowager smiled.

"You were always crazy about ships when you were a little boy," she said. "We really should have sent you into the Navy."

"I have often thought that myself," the Marquis replied. "Anyway, I am now very involved in Naval affairs."

"How is that?" the Dowager asked.

"It was when I was supervising modernisation of the Battleships in India that I received an invitation from Alexis Orestes."

"A Greek!" the Dowager exclaimed.

"A very important one," the Marquis replied. "He holds a position in Athens that I can describe only as equivalent to our First Lord of the Admiralty."

"And you had an invitation from him!" the Dowager said.

"It was more or less a command," the Marquis said as he smiled, "because in the name of the King of Greece he asked me to visit Athens on my way home from India."

"How exciting!" the Dowager murmured.

"When I arrived there, I found that the King had been advised by Orestes to order two new Battleships for the Greek Navy. He wanted them to be built in Britain, and I was to ensure that they contained all the new equipment I had talked about when I was in India."

"Oh, Guy, how splendid!" the Dowager said. "It

47

is obviously something you will enjoy doing."

"I was delighted when I was told," the Marquis said, "and there was no doubt that the Greek Navy needs bringing up-to-date."

"Then where is your problem?" the Dowager enquired.

The Marquis picked up the letter he had put on his knee.

"This is it, Grandmama," he said, "a letter I received early this morning from Orestes. I want you to translate it for me. I have an idea of what it contains, but while I can speak enough Greek to make myself understood, at least in a Restaurant, I find it extremely difficult to read."

"But surely," the Dowager said, "you have plenty of people to do that for you?"

There was a silence before the Marquis said:

"What this letter contains is, I believe, from what I can understand of it, a strictly private affair which I do not wish to be known or talked about by anyone, except my own family."

"I understand," the Dowager said quickly. "So read me the letter, Guy, and I will translate it for you."

The Marquis picked up the letter and started to read it aloud.

It was obvious to Ursa that he did not understand what he was trying to read.

Impulsively and without thinking, Ursa asked:

"Would you let me read it for you?"

The Marquis looked at her in surprise.

"You can read Greek?" he asked.

Too late Ursa knew she should have pleaded ignorance.

Penelope hated foreign languages and never made any attempt to speak them.

But before she could think of an explanation as to why she could speak Greek, the Dowager said:

"But of course Penelope can speak Greek, as well, I am sure, as many other languages. After all, Guy, you know her father is Matthew Hollington."

"Yes, of course!" the Marquis exclaimed. "I had forgotten that, and I can only say how grateful I am that you are here at this particular moment, when I need you!"

He held out the two pages of the letter as he spoke, and Ursa took them from him.

She glanced at them and saw they were written in a clear hand, and for her, at any rate, were easy to interpret.

Slowly, in her quiet, gentle voice she translated:

"My dear Marquis of Charnwood,

It gave me very great pleasure to see you when you came to Greece at my invitation, and His Majesty the King was delighted with the proposition you made and that you will personally attend to the building and outfitting of the two Battleships we have ordered.

I am now writing to you to say that at the request of Her Majesty Queen Victoria, I shall be arriving in England at about the same time as you receive this letter which I am sending via the Diplomatic Courier.

I am due at Windsor Castle on Monday, 12th,

when I have a special audience with Her Majesty.

I am however arriving on Saturday so that I can take the opportunity of accepting your very kind invitation to visit Charnwood Court.

I am bringing with me my daughter, Amelia, who is as eager as I am to see you again. I thought in Athens how admirably suited you two young people were to each other, and nothing would give me greater pleasure if, when we are at Charnwood Court, you would ask my permission to make her a member of your family.

In view of your most kind and sincere offer of hospitality, Amelia and I will arrive at your ancestral home on Saturday afternoon.

The Greek Embassy are making all the arrangements, and we look forward eagerly to being united with you again.

With the felicitations of His Majesty, and the good wishes of my wife and other members of my family,

> *I remain,*
> *Yours with deepest sincerity,*
> *Alexis Orestes."*

The Marquis stopped speaking, and for a moment there was complete silence.

Then the Dowager said:

"It is quite obvious what he is suggesting. Do you, my dear boy, wish to marry this girl?"

"No, of course not!" the Marquis said emphatically.

"But you must have given her reason to believe you were fond of her."

The Marquis made a helpless gesture with his hand.

"I was making sure, Grandmama, that the Greeks bought our Battleships. The man with the power to say yes or no to anything I suggested was Orestes. I went to see him at his home and, as you know, hospitality in Greece is very much a family affair."

He paused before he went on:

"They were all there—quite a number of them—not only his daughters and sons, but also his Grandmother, Aunts, Uncles, the whole caboodle, as well as this young woman called Amelia. She is the oldest daughter and, as she sat next to me at mealtimes, I naturally paid her compliments and set out to make myself charming."

The Marquis sighed.

"It never for one moment entered my head that he might wish his daughter to marry me!"

The Dowager smiled.

"My dear Guy, you are not only a Marquis, you are also a very attractive young man."

"At that particular time my mind was more on Battleships than women!" the Marquis said dryly.

"But *she* was thinking of *you!*"

"I see that now," the Marquis said. "Grandmama, what am I to do? I cannot refuse to see him and, if he feels insulted, he may tell the Queen on Monday that Greece will look elsewhere for her Battleships, and I will be in the 'Dog House!' "

"I see your difficulty, my poor Guy!" the Dowager said. "You are in a very unfortunate position."

"I am well aware of that!" the Marquis said unhappily.

He got to his feet as if he could not sit still, and walked to stand in front of the mantelpiece.

"It simply never occurred to me that Orestes wanted me for a son-in-law," he said, "or that his daughter should marry outside her own country."

He fell silent for a moment. Then he went on:

"Now, when I look back, I should have realised that Amelia was always with us, even when Orestes and I should have been alone. She seldom spoke, and we took no notice of her for most of the time."

"Is she pretty?" the Dowager asked.

"Not particularly," the Marquis said thoughtfully. "She is small, but rather heavily built, with an olive skin, dark hair, and not, I think, very intelligent."

The Dowager gave a horrified cry.

"In which case you cannot marry her, dear boy!"

"I know that," the Marquis replied, "but how am I to get out of it without insulting Orestes?"

There was silence.

Then Ursa said in a small voice:

"When Mr. Orestes arrives . . . could you not convince him that you are already . . . engaged to be married?"

The Marquis turned to look at Ursa as if he had never seen her before.

For a moment he did not speak.

Then he said:

"But of course! Why did not I think of that? You are brilliant—quite brilliant!"

He was quiet for a moment, as if he were working it out.

Then he said:

"But to make him believe I am not free, and realise that he cannot question it in any way, I should, of course, have my fiancée with me."

"Yes, I can see that," the Dowager agreed. "Otherwise he might think you were just making excuses not to propose to his daughter."

The Marquis put his hand up to his forehead.

"Now, whom can I produce like a rabbit out of a hat to play the part of my future wife?"

"There must be a number of young women who would be only too delighted to help you," the Dowager said with a hint of laughter in her voice. "After all, dearest Guy, I have lost count of the Beauties who have sighed over you and declared their hearts were broken when you left them."

"That is unkind, Grandmama!" the Marquis complained. "I have always believed that my *affaires de coeur* were very discreet."

The Dowager laughed.

"Gossip is carried on the wind, and I usually know about your latest *affaire*, as you call it, almost as soon as it has started."

"All I can say is that I am not involved in one at the moment," the Marquis said, "nor can I think of anyone who would be prepared to play the part whom I could trust not to talk about it afterwards."

"That would be disastrous!" the Dowager agreed. "Apart from anything else, if it reached the ears of the Queen, she would be extremely angry."

The Marquis made a helpless gesture with his hand.

"Then what can I do, Grandmama? That is why I came to you. You have never failed me when I have been in a scrape from the time I was in the Nursery until you saved me from being sent down at Oxford."

The Dowager laughed again.

"That is true, and, of course, I must save you now. But whatever happens, no-one must ever know what has occurred, so it has to be—"

She stopped.

"—Penelope!" she exclaimed. "When your Greek friends are staying in England, Penelope could be your 'fiancée' for the two nights they are at Charnwood Court!"

Ursa gave a little gasp, but before she could say anything the Marquis exclaimed:

"But of course! If she will do it, Penelope would be the perfect person."

He turned to Penelope.

"There is no reason why Orestes should ever have heard of you, let alone seen you. He has not been in England for ten years, and I know that Uncle Arthur has never been to Greece since he married! What do you say?"

"B-but . . . but . . ." Ursa murmured, "what would I have . . . to do?"

"As little as possible," the Marquis answered. "You just have to look beautiful, and when I introduce you as my fiancée, which of course we have not yet formally announced, there will be nothing Orestes can say except 'Congratulations!' "

"I . . . I am afraid I might . . . do something wrong," Ursa stammered in a small voice.

It struck her, however, that if she was acting one part, she should be able to act two.

"Do not worry, dearest child," the Dowager said. "I will be with you. At least I hope my grandson is extending the invitation to me. I would not miss this exciting drama for anything in the world!"

"Of course you are coming with me," the Marquis agreed. "You will be able to talk to Orestes in his own language and make it quite clear, sad though it is, that you will not have a Greek granddaughter."

"I . . . I suppose it is . . . all right," Ursa said.

She was speaking really to herself.

Then the Marquis stepped forward and took her hand.

"I know I am asking a great deal of you," he said in a deep voice, "but I should be very, very grateful for your help in saving me from what I know would be a disastrous marriage."

As he finished speaking, he raised her hand to his lips and kissed it.

"Thank you!" he said.

As his lips touched her skin, Ursa felt a little quiver go through her.

She thought it was one of fear.

The Marquis picked up the bottle of champagne.

There were two other glasses on the tray, and he filled all three of them.

"Now," he said, "I am going to drink to the brilliance of my Grandmother, and the kindness and understanding of my other very beautiful relative."

He raised his glass, and he was looking at Ursa as he did so.

Once again she felt that little quiver run through her.

Once again the colour was rising in her cheeks.

chapter four

WHEN morning came, Ursa hurried down for breakfast.

She found that the Marquis had finished and gone out to the stables.

It did not surprise her.

She was certain he would be as efficient in regard to his horses as her Father had always been.

She had just finished eating when she heard the Dowager talking to her maid as she led her downstairs.

She had breakfasted in her own room, and Ursa ran out to greet her in the hall.

As she did so, the Marquis came in through the front-door.

"Good-morning, Grandmama!" he said. "I hope it is not too tiring for you to get up so early."

"Not at all!" the Dowager replied. "I am looking forward to the drive, and being at Charnwood Court again."

The Marquis kissed her cheek.

"You are wonderful," he said, "and you know how important you are to me."

He paused before he went on:

"Because I want to be ahead of you to welcome you when you arrive, I am riding over on one of your best horses."

"Riding?" the Dowager exclaimed.

"Yes, Grandmama, and you and Penelope will go in the Travelling Carriage in which I came. My coachman is a good driver, although he will take a little longer to get back to Charnwood than I did to get here."

"It sounds delightful!" the Dowager said.

To Ursa's surprise, as the Marquis drew his Grandmother into the Drawing-Room, he said to her:

"Come with us."

When they were inside he shut the door before he said:

"We should decide before we leave what to call Penelope."

"I have been thinking about that," the Dowager replied. "In order to avoid any confusion, I suggest it would make things easier if she uses the name of her younger sister."

"Her sister?" the Marquis exclaimed. "I did not know she had one."

"Matthew Hollington has two daughters—Penelope, who is the elder, and Ursa."

She smiled before she added:

" 'Ursa' also is Greek and it means 'Nymph of the Sea.' What could be more appropriate, Guy, when all this is about Battleships?"

The Marquis chuckled.

"That is true, and of course it is perfect for my fiancée to have a Greek name, although I am not certain Orestes will appreciate that."

Because what he said sounded funny, Ursa laughed.

She thought that nothing could be more ridiculous than that she was now reverting to being herself for Mr. Orestes, while still pretending to be Penelope to the Marquis and his Grandmother.

"That is settled, then," the Marquis said, "and the sooner you get off, the better! I promise that although your luncheon will be late, it will be a good one."

"Thank you, dearest boy," the Dowager replied, "and do not worry about me. I assure you I feel twenty years younger, as something exciting is happening!"

As they walked through the hall, Ursa thought that was certainly true.

Her Father had always said it was a great mistake for a man or woman to retire too early.

"They then sit about doing nothing," he had added, "until they die. It is better to keep not only our bodies, but also our brains occupied."

The Travelling Carriage in which the Marquis had arrived was a spectacular vehicle and extremely comfortable.

It was drawn by four horses that were perfectly matched.

The elderly coachman on the box raised his cockaded hat as Ursa and the Dowager climbed in.

Behind them was a Brake on which the luggage

was being loaded by the footmen.

Ursa could also see Marie, and Martha, the Dowager's maid, sitting inside it.

She had told Marie while she was dressing what was happening.

That still posing as Penelope, she must now pretend to Mr. Orestes to be her sister Ursa, and the fiancée of the Marquis.

Being French, Marie accepted the situation without surprise or consternation.

"I am sure that as my sister has never been to Charnwood Court," Ursa added, "we need not worry about the staff there."

"Not while I have been with her, M'Lady," Marie answered. *"Voilà!* Now I must go back to calling you *M'mselle* instead of 'M'Lady!' "

"I am quite used to that," Ursa replied.

As they drove off, she said to the Dowager:

"This is certainly an adventure, and it will be interesting to see Charnwood Court."

"It is a very beautiful house," the Dowager said, "and has been in the Charn family for generations. Guy is only the third Marquis, but the Charns go back to Elizabethan times, and the Earldom is a very old one."

They went a little further before the Dowager said:

"As you have never met Guy before, I suspect Arthur has not told you about him."

"No . . . he has . . . not," Ursa replied.

She wondered what there was to tell.

She was afraid she might make a mistake about what Penelope would know about him.

"Then I think I should tell you," the Dowager said, "that he is not really my grandson."

Ursa turned her head to look at the Dowager in surprise.

"Not your grandson?" she queried, "but . . . he calls you 'Grandmama.' "

"Yes, I know," the Dowager agreed, "and we do not usually bother to make explanations to people. But, of course, as you are one of the family, it is different."

"Then . . . why is he not your grandson?" Ursa asked.

The Dowager settled herself more comfortably in her padded seat before she said:

"He is, to be exact, my step-grandson. My first child after I married was Arthur. It was some years later that I had a daughter who I christened Charlotte."

"Such a pretty name!" Ursa murmured.

"She was very pretty," the Dowager went on, "but she married a man much older than herself, who was the Marquis of Charnwood."

She smiled as she continued:

"He was, as you can imagine, a very attractive, handsome man, but he had been married before."

Ursa was listening intently as the Dowager went on:

"It had been an arranged marriage, and I gather not a very happy one. His wife died of pneumonia when their son was only a year old."

Ursa was beginning to understand what had happened, but she did not say anything.

"Guy was seven when his Father married Charlotte. He had been brought up by various relatives and was thrilled to have a real home. He adored Charlotte and soon called her 'Mama,' as if she were really his mother."

"And did not your daughter have any children of her own?" Ursa asked.

"Oh, yes," the Dowager replied. "She had three daughters, but the eldest was not born until they had been married for four years. This was somewhat of a disappointment, but in any case, Guy was the rightful heir to the title."

"And . . . are the daughters . . . grown up?" Ursa asked nervously.

She was thinking that perhaps Penelope had met them, and if they were at Charnwood, they would be suspicious of her, although, of course, she was now Ursa.

They would not know unless they were told that she had been pretending to be her sister.

"They are still at school, but the eldest will make her debut next year," the Dowager was saying.

Ursa gave a little sigh of relief knowing she had nothing to fear from the Marquis's half-sisters.

At the same time, she thought it was sad that he had never known his own Mother.

"I have always thought," the Dowager said quietly, "that Arthur has somewhat resented Guy adopting me as his Grandmother. But he was not happy as a small boy, and I have always loved him."

"That does not surprise me," Ursa replied, "because he is so good-looking."

She thought again she had never seen a man who was so handsome.

She wished she could see him on a horse,

because she was sure that was how he would look his best.

"And where is your daughter now?" Ursa asked.

She was suddenly afraid she might be at Charnwood Court.

"She is in Somerset," the Dowager replied, "in a house where she has lived since her husband died. Guy often goes to see her, but I think that since Charlotte has children of her own, he really feels more at home with me."

The Travelling Carriage was now moving very fast, which made it difficult for them to talk.

After a while the Dowager shut her eyes and appeared to be asleep.

It was then that Ursa could think about herself.

Nothing, she thought, could be more exciting than what was taking place.

'If I do not make any mistakes,' she told herself, 'it will be something to remember all my life as an adventure greater than any I had on my journeys with Papa!'

*   *   *

The Travelling Carriage turned in at a pair of very fine wrought-iron gates at exactly twenty minutes past one o'clock.

There was a long drive up to the house with huge oak trees on either side of it.

Then Ursa saw Charnwood Court for the first time and gave a little cry of delight.

She might have known, she thought, that it would be exactly the right frame and background for the Marquis.

It was very large, and the central block of the building had a tower on which was flying the Marquis's flag.

On either side were two wings, which looked as if they had subsequently been added, but in harmony with the original.

It stood on high ground, and below it lay a lake on which, as they crossed the bridge, Ursa saw a number of swans.

The gardens around the house were ablaze with colour.

The green lawns that sloped down to the lake were like velvet.

'It is a Palace,' she thought, 'fit for Prince Charming, who is the Marquis himself.'

He was waiting for them at the top of the steps that led to the main entrance.

When the Travelling Carriage came to a standstill he ran down the red carpet to open the carriage door before a footman could do so.

"Welcome to Charnwood Court, Grandmama!" he said. "I cannot tell you how delighted I am to have you here again."

"And I am delighted to be here, dear boy," the Dowager said.

The Marquis helped her out of the carriage, then smiled at Ursa as she followed him.

"It is delightful to see you again, Ursa!" he said.

He raised his voice a little so that the footman, who had hurried down the steps after him, would hear.

"I too am . . . delighted to be . . . here," Ursa managed to say.

The Marquis led the Dowager up the steps and into what Ursa saw was a magnificent hall.

There was a crystal and bronze staircase, and opposite it a huge marble fireplace on each side of which hung flags.

Ursa guessed they were those the Charns had collected in battle.

The Marquis guided the Dowager into a very large and exquisitely furnished room.

There was a bottle of champagne cooling on ice, and a housemaid to help them off with their travelling-clothes.

"I thought you would not wish to go upstairs straight away, after such a long journey," the Marquis said, "but if you wish to take off your hats, which I am sure you do, there is a room opening out of this one, where there are plenty of mirrors in which to admire yourselves!"

The Dowager laughed.

"I remember that, Guy, and always thought it very convenient."

She and Ursa went into the room he indicated, washed their hands, and took off their hats.

"Now I feel more comfortable," the Dowager said, "and it is like Guy to think of everything."

"He is certainly very considerate," Ursa agreed, "and I hope we shall have a delicious luncheon, for quite frankly I am very hungry!"

The Dowager laughed.

"When I last came to Charnwood I put on pounds in weight because the food was so appetising!"

"That is a very comforting thought at the moment," Ursa replied.

The food was indeed delicious and served in the most impressive Dining-Room that Ursa had ever seen.

There was a Minstrels' Gallery at one end.

On the walls were magnificent portraits of the Marquis's ancestors.

She thought that, sitting at the head of the table, he resembled many of them.

In fact, he was even more handsome than those who had been painted by Van Dyck.

Because she was genuinely curious, the Marquis told her quite a lot about the pictures and finished by saying:

"I must show you the Picture Gallery. My father's hobby was to collect paintings from all over the world. As a small boy I felt as if I had visited Venice and many parts of the East simply because I had looked so often at the pictures illustrating them, and heard them described to me by my Governess."

"That was what my Father did to me," Ursa said.

Just in time she prevented herself from adding that she had visited many of the places with her Father.

She was not aware that the Marquis was surprised at how knowledgeable she was about the Artists of whom he was speaking.

He was finding also that he could talk to her about the places he had visited and that she was really interested in what he was saying.

She was not just pretending to be, as so many other women had done in the past.

After luncheon he insisted that his Grandmother should go upstairs and rest.

"I have ascertained that Orestes, coming by train, should be here about four o'clock," he said. "That is when you will have to help me, Grandmama, so I hope you will try to sleep before it is time to come down."

"I do not intend to argue on that subject," the Dowager said as she smiled. "I will simply do as I am told!"

The Marquis guided her upstairs.

When they had gone, Ursa had time to inspect the room in which they had been before luncheon.

There were some delightful pictures on the walls and also a collection of snuff-boxes which she knew must be very valuable.

She was gazing at a fine Rembrandt when the Marquis came back.

"We now have a short time in which to enjoy ourselves before the drama begins," he stated. "What would you like to do?"

"There is so much I want to see," Ursa replied. "And as I am so afraid of missing something important, I am hesitating between the Picture Gallery and the stables."

The Marquis laughed.

"That is exactly the answer which in the circumstances I would have given myself. If we hurry, we may be able to do both, so let us start with the stables."

When Ursa saw the horses she realised that although he had been away for some time and had only just returned, he had kept in touch with his Manager.

The horses he had left behind might have grown

older, but they were in every way magnificent.

"How could you bear to leave them?" she asked as she went from stall to stall.

"I admit that when I was given some half-bred hack to ride, it made me feel homesick," the Marquis replied. "But now I am home for good, and I intend to build up my racing stable as well as add to the horses I have here."

"I think they are perfect," Ursa said admiringly.

He shook his head.

"I need yearlings, and I also need what is very important, Arab blood."

Ursa gave a little sigh.

She thought of how her Father, in a limited way, for he was not a very rich man, had kept an excellent stable of horses.

She might perhaps have been bored with the country, like Penelope, if she had not been able to ride.

"We will ride to-morrow morning," the Marquis said, "and we can only hope that Orestes will not wish to join us—nor his daughter!"

"That would be wonderful!" Ursa said.

"I do not know why," the Marquis said as they walked back to the house, "but I always had the idea when they talked about your beauty that you were not a very enthusiastic horsewoman."

Too late, much too late, Ursa remembered that while Penelope rode occasionally in the Park because it was fashionable, she had never enjoyed hunting.

She had always preferred to be driven about in one of her Father's carriages than to mount a horse.

"I enjoy riding," she said quickly, "but only when I have horses as good as yours."

It was a lame excuse, but the Marquis seemed to accept it.

Ursa quickly went on to speak about the pictures they were to see.

They were certainly magnificent.

The Picture Gallery stretched the whole length of one of the wings.

They went from one picture to another.

It was only with the greatest of difficulty that Ursa prevented herself from saying that she had been in this place or that, when looking at a wonderful reproduction of what she had actually seen.

Only when the Marquis looked at his watch did she realise how long they had taken and how interesting it had all been.

"Is it time for them to arrive?" she asked.

"They should be here in about ten minutes," the Marquis replied. "Perhaps we had better go downstairs and be waiting in the Drawing-Room."

When Ursa saw it, she realised that the Marquis obviously intended to impress the Greek. It was certainly the most spectacular room in the house.

It was massed with white orchids and other exotic plants which had come from the Himalayas, and she exclaimed in delight.

She knew that the moment was near when she would be introduced as the Marquis's fiancée.

It was then she said:

"I wonder if perhaps I should have changed my gown. I never thought of it until this moment."

"You look very lovely as you are!" the Marquis said. "And shall I tell you that I am astonished at how unselfconscious you appear to be about your looks? Unlike most other women, you do not seem to keep worrying about your appearance."

There was a note of sincerity in his voice that made her feel rather shy.

She could not, of course, explain that she did not worry about her looks because she had never thought of herself as a great beauty.

When she travelled with her Father she felt that no-one noticed particularly what she was wearing.

"You are very beautiful," the Marquis said in a low voice, "as of course a million men must already have told you, but there is something else about you that I did not expect."

"What is . . . that?" Ursa asked nervously.

The Marquis was just about to reply, when the door opened and the Butler announced:

"Mr. Alexis Orestes, M'Lord, and Miss Amelia Orestes!"

He pronounced the names in such a strange way that Ursa wanted to laugh.

They were standing by the mantelpiece.

The Marquis hurried across the room, holding out his hand.

Alexis Orestes was not very tall, but he had an intelligent expression, and he looked unmistakably Greek.

His daughter was short, rather heavily-built as the Marquis had said, and obviously very young.

She was not at all attractive, nor was she very smartly dressed.

The Marquis greeted his guests enthusiastically.

"I am delighted to welcome you to Charnwood!" he was saying. "I am so glad that you thought of coming here."

He shook Alexis Orestes's hand, then turned to Amelia.

"I hope you had a good journey," he said, "and that you are not too tired?"

"I am not tired, thank you," the Greek girl answered, speaking quite fluent English.

The Marquis turned back towards the fireplace.

"My Grandmother is here with me," he said, "and will be coming downstairs later. But now I want you to meet someone who is very special to me, and I want you to be among the first to congratulate me."

There was a question in the Greek's dark eyes as he looked at the Marquis enquiringly.

As they reached Ursa, the Marquis was saying:

"Allow me to introduce you to Miss Ursa Hollington, who is the daughter of Matthew Hollington, the distinguished Linguist of whom I am sure you have heard."

He smiled at her and then said:

"Miss Hollington has made me the most fortunate man in the world, and it was only a day or two before I received your letter."

Ursa held out her hand, and as the Greek took it he said:

"I do not understand!"

"You are the first of my friends to be told that Ursa has agreed to become my wife," the Marquis said. "I know that you will give us your blessing and drink our health in champagne."

He turned towards the table on which the champagne stood before the Greek could speak.

It had been brought in before the guests arrived.

Ursa knew this was because he had no wish for the servants to learn about his "engagement."

As he poured the champagne into the glasses he went on:

"I have told you this in complete confidence, and I would be grateful if you do not mention it to anyone, as we have yet to inform our relatives. They are scattered everywhere, so it will take time."

He handed a glass of champagne first to Alexis Orestes and then to his daughter.

It was obvious to Ursa that the Greek was disappointed and a little disconcerted.

However, she did not think he was particularly angry.

She glanced at his daughter, Amelia.

She did not seem at all upset that she had lost the man her Father had chosen for her.

Ursa wondered if she had even been consulted as to whether she wished to marry him.

The Marquis put a glass of champagne into Ursa's hand, then lifted his own.

"To you, Alexis Orestes," he said, "and may you continue to be as successful in the future as you already are, and impress Queen Victoria when you meet her on Monday!"

The Greek managed to laugh.

"I doubt if anybody could do that!" he said. "Your

Queen and her Empire represent the pinnacle of power, and who could possibly challenge that?"

The Marquis laughed.

"I assure you, a great number of people would like to try."

"Only to be defeated!" the Greek said. "And may that continue to be the case for a very long time."

It was a compliment, and the Marquis said:

"We have much to be proud of in our Empire, but who can match the entrancing History of Ancient Greece, and, of course, the possession of Mount Olympus?"

Alexis Orestes laughed.

"That is true."

Because she felt she should say something, Ursa said:

"My Father loves Greece and taught me when I was a child to speak your language."

She was speaking in Greek, and Alexis Orestes said:

"That is splendid! You speak very fluently! I am surprised!"

"It is such a lovely language," Ursa said, "and I feel so privileged to be able to read the works of your great Authors."

Alexis Orestes was obviously intrigued.

He sat down beside Ursa on the sofa and they conversed together in his language.

Ursa was glad that the Marquis could not understand what was said.

She could not help telling Alexis Orestes that she had been to Greece and seen much that was beautiful there.

This was something that Penelope had not done.

But Ursa thought that if later Alexis Orestes was to mention to the Marquis that she had been in his country, he would not be suspicious.

He would merely think she was being clever in saying she had done what she knew Ursa had done.

After they had finished the champagne, the Marquis took Alexis Orestes to his Study.

Ursa guessed he would take the opportunity to discuss business.

Left alone with Amelia, Ursa found her difficult to talk to, even though they were speaking in her language.

"Tell me about yourself," she asked. "What do you do when you are in Athens? Do you attend many Balls?"

"I go to some parties," Amelia answered, "but they are nearly always given by Papa's friends, and those I meet are as old as he is."

Ursa laughed.

"That must be very boring for you! But surely there are many young men in Athens, and you must have many friends among them?"

"No, not many," Amelia said. "Papa wishes me to marry someone who is important, but the men who are important in my country are usually very old."

Ursa was beginning to understand.

This was why Alexis Orestes had set his heart on having the Marquis as a son-in-law.

She dared not say that to Amelia in case it was repeated, and instead she said:

"I expect you would like to come upstairs and rest a little before dinner."

"I would like that," Amelia answered. "I have a headache from travelling in the train and listening to Papa, who talked and talked!"

"What about?" Ursa asked.

There was a little silence.

Then Amelia replied:

"He was instructing me about what I should say and what I should not say when I met the Marquis again. But now that he is to marry you, Papa must look elsewhere for a suitable husband for me."

Ursa looked at the Greek girl in surprise.

"But surely you do not have to marry anyone you do not want to?"

"I have to marry whom Papa chooses," Amelia said.

She spoke firmly.

Ursa was aware that she accepted there would be no argument about it.

"Let us go upstairs," she said quickly, feeling it would be a mistake to say any more.

She took Amelia upstairs, then went to her own bed-room.

She found it was a lovely room, with a *Boudoir* opening out of it.

In fact, it was the most impressive bed-room she had ever imagined she would be sleeping in.

Marie, having unpacked her clothes, was nowhere to be seen.

She therefore went out into the corridor, wondering where the Dowager's room was to be found.

As she did so, a housemaid came hurrying along the corridor, and she asked:

"Can you tell me where Lady Brackley is sleeping?"

The housemaid dropped a little curtsy.

"Yes, Miss," she replied. "Her Ladyship's in the room opposite, but when I looks a little while ago, she was fast asleep, an' I thought it would be a mistake t' wake her."

"You were quite right," Ursa said, knowing this was the reason the Dowager had not come downstairs.

She went back to her own room.

Going into the *Boudoir*, she found there were some extremely interesting books which she knew she would enjoy.

One was a history of the house, with illustrations.

It was so fascinating that Ursa sat down on the sofa.

She had been reading for nearly half-an-hour when the door opened and the Marquis came in.

He shut the door behind him and said:

"I might have known I would find you here!"

Ursa looked up at him with a smile, and he sat down beside her on the sofa.

"It has all gone off perfectly!" he said.

"Your Greek friend did not say he was disappointed?"

The Marquis shook his head.

"He is too diplomatic for that! He merely congratulated me on marrying anyone so beautiful. Then we talked business."

"His daughter told me that her Father was intent on marrying her to someone important, and that she had no choice in the matter!"

"Poor girl!" the Marquis exclaimed.

"She also said," Ursa went on, "that her Father instructed her all the way here in the train how she should behave and what she should say to you. I think she finds it a great relief that she need say nothing."

The Marquis looked at her for a moment before he asked:

"How can I thank you for not only thinking of anything so clever, but of carrying it off so brilliantly?"

Ursa gave a little sigh.

" 'Touch wood!' " she begged. "We must still be very careful not to make any mistakes."

"That is true," the Marquis agreed. "Orestes is very clever and charming, but he would also be extremely ruthless if he discovered he had been deceived and resented it."

"Then we must not put a foot wrong until he leaves for London."

The Marquis was looking at Ursa. Then he asked:

"How can you be so beautiful and so clever? I have known many women, but none of them had your intelligence. Nor could they speak Greek so fluently! Orestes was extremely impressed."

"It was just your good luck!" Ursa said.

"I must go back now," the Marquis said, "and continue to make myself pleasant. I came upstairs really to find out if Grandmama was coming down, but I gather she is still asleep. I have told the maid not to wake her until it is time to change for dinner."

"That is very sensible," Ursa said.

"And you are not only sensible, but also exceptional," the Marquis said softly.

He rose to his feet as he spoke, and Ursa looked up at him.

Their eyes met, and it was impossible for either of them to look away.

Then, abruptly, as if he forced himself to do so, the Marquis turned and walked towards the door.

chapter five

URSA ran down the stairs at seven o'clock next morning feeling like a School-girl playing truant.

She was sure the Dowager was fast asleep, as were the Greeks.

At the same time, she had the guilty feeling that she should not be going out riding with the Marquis.

It was, however, something she knew would be exciting.

It would be something to remember when she rode her Father's horses which, although good, did not compare with the Marquis's.

Last night had not been as difficult as she had feared.

She had set herself out to be charming to Alexis Orestes.

He had responded to her knowledge of Greece and the compliments she paid him on his distinguished position.

It was easier to talk in his language so that the

Marquis did not understand what they were saying.

She found the Greek was extremely knowledge-able on Greek History.

She also discovered he had a collection of Greek sculptures which she would have loved to see.

When they went up to bed, the Marquis escorted his Grandmother to the foot of the stairs.

As the Greeks had not yet followed them, he said to Ursa:

"Well done! You were absolutely splendid, and you know how grateful I am."

There was no time to say any more because Alexis Orestes and his daughter had now joined them.

Ursa guided the Dowager up the stairs and into her bed-room.

Her maid was waiting for her.

Instead of saying anything, Ursa just kissed Lady Brackley good-night, and went to her own room.

She realised when she reached it that she was tired.

But she was not as worried or as anxious as she had been before the Greeks arrived.

She fell asleep thinking only of the Marquis.

Somehow he seemed to fill her dreams so that she was still thinking of him when she woke up.

Now she went out of the front-door and saw that the horses were waiting.

The Marquis was standing beside the one with a side-saddle.

It was then she realised that he had had the fore-sight to arrange that none of the guests bed-rooms were at the front of the house.

As he lifted her onto her mount she felt a little quiver run through her.

She thought it was relief that no-one was with them.

As they crossed the bridge that spanned the lake, she was sure no-one had seen them go.

The Marquis's horse was very frisky, and as they rode towards some level ground he said:

"I suggest we gallop some of the exuberance out of our animals, provided that you are satisfied with yours?"

"I am more than satisfied," Ursa replied.

She knew from the way the Marquis was looking that he was hoping the horse would not prove too much for her.

Perhaps he expected that she would just want to "trit-trot."

That, as she was told, was what the Ladies in London, like Penelope, did in Hyde Park.

She knew her sister would never think of galloping, if she could avoid it.

The Marquis had been correct in his assumption that Penelope was not a keen rider.

Although Ursa told herself it was a mistake, she could not resist setting off at a tremendous speed.

They rode for nearly a mile before they started to pull in their mounts.

Ursa turned then to look at the Marquis.

Her cheeks were flushed, her eyes shining.

Although she was unaware of it, she looked even more lovely than ever.

"That was marvellous!" she exclaimed.

"And so are you," the Marquis replied. "I had no idea you rode so well."

"I have ridden since I could walk," Ursa told him without thinking.

"Then why are your stables not filled with horses as good as these?"

His question brought Ursa back to reality with a bang.

She remembered she was supposed to be Penelope, the wife of a wealthy man.

She gave a little shrug of her shoulders.

"Arthur does not often ride these days. He cannot find the time for it."

She had thought of saying that he was too old, but decided it would sound unkind.

At the same time, she had to find some excuse, as it was quite obvious the Marquis knew she did not ride regularly.

They went on through the woods.

Then they climbed to the top of some high ground so that the Marquis could show Ursa the extent of his Estate.

It was very beautiful, and Ursa said as she looked at it:

"You must be very proud of owning so much! But I realise it is a great responsibility."

The Marquis looked at her in surprise.

"What do you mean by that?" he asked.

"There is not only so much land which is yours, but also the people who live on it are yours too, and I am sure they look to you for guidance and help."

She was simply saying what came into her mind.

There was a moment's pause before the Marquis answered:

"Are you really rebuking me for having been abroad for so long and not acting like a shepherd in watching over my people?"

"I was not thinking that at all," Ursa replied. "However, it is an excellent definition of what every good Landlord should be."

"I suppose I wanted, while I am young," the Marquis said, "to see the world and, if you like, enjoy myself before I am troubled with too much responsibility."

The way he spoke made Ursa think of how unhappy he had been when he was a little boy.

"I was not really rebuking you," she said quickly, "and everything I have seen at Charnwood is perfect! I should, in fact, be congratulating you."

"It is the way my Father left it, and the way I intend Charnwood to continue," the Marquis said firmly, "but I also want it to be a home."

Ursa remembered how the Dowager had told her that was what he had lacked.

It was why he had been thrilled when his Father had married again.

"Of course you want a home," she said gently, "and lots of children to enjoy your magnificent house and ride your marvellous horses."

The Marquis laughed.

"You are going too fast. At the same time, I would like to teach my sons to shoot and my daughters to ride as well as you do."

"I am sure that is what you will do," Ursa said. "According to your Grandmother, there are a great number of beautiful young women longing to be offered the position of chatelaine of Charnwood Court."

She was speaking lightly, but the Marquis said in a serious tone:

"I have first to fall in love."

"Surely that is not difficult?" Ursa asked.

"It might be very difficult if it was with the wrong person," the Marquis replied.

He spoke in a sharp tone and turned his horse as he did so in the direction from which they had come.

Then he added:

"I think we should be going back."

Feeling she had said something wrong, Ursa felt worried as she followed him.

As they were on a narrow path through some trees, she was unable to ride beside him.

When they reached the open, the Marquis began to ride swiftly, as if he was eager to get back.

"What . . . have I . . . said? What have . . . I done?" Ursa asked herself.

As she went over their conversation in her mind, she decided he must be in love already, obviously with someone he could not marry.

'I want him to be happy,' she thought. 'He is so kind, so considerate, that he deserves to have exactly what he wants.'

The Marquis slowed down when they were only a short distance from the house.

"Have you enjoyed your ride?" he asked.

"It has been very exciting," Ursa said. "I do hope I have a chance to ride one of your horses again before we leave."

"There is no hurry for you and Grandmama to do so," the Marquis answered. "Orestes told me last night that he wants to catch an early train tomorrow morning so that he and his daughter have time for luncheon before they drive down to Windsor Castle."

"I am sure from what he said last night," Ursa said, "that he will give a very glowing account to Her Majesty of the advice you have given for modernising the Greek Navy and your promise to help with supervision."

"I hope so," the Marquis replied, "but I realise it is all due to you that I do not have to have a Greek wife."

"If you were having one," Ursa remarked, "I think she should look like a Greek Goddess from Olympus, because Charnwood deserves nothing less."

"Actually, I was thinking of Diana the Huntress," the Marquis said.

"That is very ambitious!" Ursa laughed.

She looked at the Marquis as she did so, then realised he was paying her a compliment.

Once again their eyes met, then suddenly feeling shy, Ursa looked away.

She spurred her horse to move faster, and they arrived back at the stables in silence.

When the Marquis lifted her down from the saddle, she again felt a little thrill run through her.

Then she told herself she was being stupid.

Any other woman, she thought, would take his compliments at face value.

Because she was so countrified, she felt shy.

She blushed, which was something she was certain her sister would never have done.

Now she said to the Marquis:

"Thank you so much."

She turned to the Head Groom to say how fine the horses were, and he was obviously pleased at her appreciation.

The Marquis started giving some orders as to what he wanted for the rest of the day.

Ursa hurried back into the house without waiting.

She thought it would be a mistake for the Dowager to hear that she had been riding alone with the Marquis.

She, if no-one else, would be aware that it was something Penelope would not have done.

Penelope had always disliked getting up early, apart from the fact that she had no wish to ride.

"I must be careful, very, very careful!" Ursa told herself as she went up the stairs to her bed-room.

* * *

The rest of the day passed very successfully.

The Marquis had tentatively suggested taking the Greeks round the house in the morning.

After that they had had an early luncheon before they went for a drive over the Estate.

He pointed out the beauty spots which Ursa knew could in no way compare with the grandeur of mountain scenery in Greece.

He took them to a farm, and Alexis Orestes was extremely interested in the modern implements the Marquis had introduced.

He wanted also to know how much the crops sold for.

Ursa thought the Greek thought of everything only in terms of money, being first and foremost a businessman.

When they returned to the house where the Dowager was waiting for them, there was champagne to drink.

There were also some *pâté* sandwiches in case they were hungry before dinner.

The only person who did not seem to have anything much to say was Amelia.

Ursa decided, although she confessed it was unkind, that she was in fact a very dull young woman.

"How could somebody like that possibly marry the Marquis?" she asked herself. "He would not only be bored, but, considering how handsome he is, there would inevitably be other women attracted to him."

She found herself wondering what the Marquis felt about the women with whom he had been talked about in London.

There were also those he had met in India and other parts of the world.

As she joined the Dowager before dinner, almost as if she read Ursa's thoughts, Lady Brackley said:

"I notice that young Greek woman has very little to say for herself, and I can only thank you a thousand times for having saved my precious Guy from a loveless marriage."

"I was thinking the same thing," Ursa said. "He must find someone really charming."

"Someone like yourself, my dearest Penelope," the Dowager said. "I was thinking only to-day how very fortunate Arthur is to have a wife like you. You are so clever with Mr. Orestes that I feel now he does not resent in any way the fact that Guy has escaped his clutches."

"I am hoping that is so," Ursa said, "and of course it is very fortunate that I can talk to him in his own language."

"I thought it was almost a miracle," the Dowager said. "Although I could not hear what you were saying because you were at the other end of the room, I knew he was laughing, and he no longer had that rather tight, resentful note in his voice which he had immediately after he arrived and found that Guy already had a fiancée."

Ursa thought, as she had before, that because the Dowager was blind, she was more sensitive to people's voices, their feelings, and especially their vibrations.

"It is important," she said aloud, "that Mr. Orestes should praise the Marquis to Her Majesty, and I feel sure that is what he will do."

"I feel the same," the Dowager said, "and it is all due to you, dearest child."

Ursa left the Dowager in the care of her lady's-maid and walked to her own room.

She was wishing that when she returned home she could still see Lady Brackley.

But she knew it would be impossible, and certainly something which Penelope would not tolerate.

It then struck her that she would also never be

able to see the Marquis again.

She was conscious of a sudden constriction in her heart.

"I want to see him," she told herself. "I want to hear his voice. I want to know that he is happy."

Because such thoughts frightened her, she hurriedly talked to Marie about what she should wear for dinner.

The dinner was an enjoyable one with the Marquis making them laugh.

Alexis Orestes said when it was time to go to bed that he had enjoyed himself enormously.

"As soon as you are married, my dear Marquis, perhaps on your honeymoon, you and your wife must come and stay with me. She is so knowledge-able about our Greek Temples, and I have many interesting relics to show her."

Ursa drew in her breath, knowing he had implied that she had been to Greece.

The Marquis did not seem to notice, however, and he merely replied:

"Of course, that is something we would be delighted to do, and anyway, I shall have to come to Greece sooner or later to consult with you over the Battleships."

"I shall look forward to it with the greatest pleasure," Mr. Orestes said.

He bade the Dowager good-night, then turned to Ursa, saying:

"You are so beautiful, Miss Hollington, that I know when you visit me every Sculptor in Greece will want to make a statue of you, and every Artist paint your portrait."

"You are very kind, but nobody could compete with the beauties of Ancient Greece which you already possess."

She kissed Amelia good-bye, saying:

"I shall hope to see you in the morning, if I do not oversleep."

As she went upstairs with the Dowager, she thought with a sigh of relief that it was over.

There had been no difficulties, no problems, and the Marquis was safe.

When Marie left Ursa she did not blow out the candles by her bedside.

Instead, she opened the book she had found in the Library about the Charn family and the house.

She had already read most of it, but there was still a number of pages left.

She wanted not only to read every word, but also to remember them.

She read ten pages and was just thinking she would leave the rest until tomorrow.

Suddenly she heard the communicating-door into the *Boudoir* open.

She looked up in surprise as she saw the Marquis coming into the room.

He shut the door behind him.

Then, as he walked forward, she saw that he was wearing a long robe which reached to the floor.

It was frogged across the chest which gave him a somewhat military appearance.

As he came towards her she gave a little gasp:

"What has happened . . . what is wrong?"

"There is nothing wrong," the Marquis answered, "but I thought I would come and say good-night to you and thank you again for making a success of what might have been a disaster."

He reached the bed as he spoke and sat down on the side of it, so that he was facing her.

The candles were shining on her hair which fell over her shoulders nearly to her waist.

As the Marquis looked at her, she suddenly felt shy and embarrassed.

"Y-you should . . . not be . . . h-here . . . it is d-dangerous!" she stammered.

"Everybody is fast asleep by now," he answered, "and I was half afraid you would be the same."

"I am . . . glad that . . . everything has gone so well . . . for you," Ursa said. "However . . . we must not take . . . any chances."

"I want to thank you now," the Marquis said, "and actually, it is something I have been wanting to do for a very long time."

He bent forward as he spoke.

Before Ursa could realise what was happening, he pressed her back against the pillows, and his lips were on hers.

For a moment she could not believe it was happening.

Then, as his lips held hers captive, she felt as if a streak of lightning ran through her body.

She had never been kissed.

Yet it was exactly what she believed a kiss would be, but infinitely more marvellous.

Because he felt her lips trembling beneath his, the Marquis drew her closer.

His kiss became more possessive and more passionate.

Suddenly Ursa felt his hand touching her breast.

She realised what was happening and struggled against him.

With a superhuman effort she turned her face away, saying as she did so:

"No . . . oh, no! You must not . . . do this . . . please . . . no!"

"Why should we pretend?" the Marquis asked. "I want you, and I think you want me."

"B-but you . . . must not . . . k-kiss me," Ursa gasped incoherently.

"I cannot think why you should say that," the Marquis argued. "After all, Lionel told me of the delightful week-end you spent together when Arthur was in Berlin, and I do not believe that Lionel is the first man to have been so fortunate."

There was a touch of cynicism in his voice.

It made Ursa realise that he was thinking of her as Penelope.

And what Penelope had done in the past she was doing again at this moment.

Because she was shocked when she thought of her sister, Ursa struggled again.

"Please . . . go away!" she begged. "Go away . . . at once! Y-you are not . . . to t-touch me . . . you are . . . not to . . . k-kiss me!"

"I cannot believe that you mean that," the Marquis said, "and although you are playing 'hard to get,' we may never have such a perfect opportunity again. Moreover, most beautiful Penelope, I find you irresistible!"

Perhaps it was being called by her sister's name that gave Ursa the strength she had not had before.

She was still feeling dazed and a little bewildered by the wonder of his kiss.

But now she put both hands against his chest.

"No . . . no!" she cried.

"And I say 'Yes! Yes,' " the Marquis retorted.

Again his lips were seeking hers.

She was suddenly aware of how strong he was and that she was helpless.

She struggled, but he was now lying on top of the bed and pulling her determinedly against him.

His arms were tightly round her.

It was then Ursa knew what he intended and that she had to save herself.

Otherwise she would be behaving in the same way that Penelope did.

With a cry that was like that of a child, she pleaded:

"P-please . . . listen to . . . me! There is . . . no one to h-help me . . . and I am . . . frightened!"

For the first time the Marquis was still.

"Frightened?" he questioned. "Why should you be frightened?"

Looking down at her, he saw that her eyes were filled with tears which were beginning to roll down her cheeks.

"I . . . I am . . . f-frightened . . . because y-you are . . . so . . . strong . . . and I do not . . . know how to s-stop y-you," Ursa managed to stammer.

"Why should you want to stop me?" the Marquis asked.

"Because . . . what you . . . want me . . . to . . . d-do is . . . wrong . . . and . . . w-wicked!"

The words came without her thinking about them.

The Marquis stared at her in sheer astonishment.

"Wrong and wicked?" he repeated. "Why should you say that?"

"It is . . . I know it . . . is," Ursa sobbed, "and I do . . . not know . . . how to . . . make you . . . understand."

"What am I supposed to understand?" the Marquis asked.

Because he thought of her as Penelope, Ursa knew she could not answer that question.

She therefore said, as the tears ran down her cheeks:

"Please . . . please . . . leave me . . . I cannot . . . explain . . . but . . . you must . . . go away!"

"I do not understand," the Marquis said. "You are very different from what I expected, but I still hoped—as I had heard a great deal about you."

He spoke as if he were speaking to himself.

Although his arms were still round her, he was not holding her so tightly, but his face was very near to hers.

Quite suddenly he said in a different tone of voice:

"I will be very gentle, and let me explain to you, my Darling, that I want you unbearably!"

Ursa looked at him through her tears.

"I . . . I cannot . . . let you . . . do what . . . you . . . want," she whispered, "because—"

She was just about to say that she was not Penelope.

Then she knew she would be betraying her sister.

That would be wrong, and something she must never do.

94

She gave a little sob before she said:

"G-go away . . . please . . . go away . . . there is . . . nothing I can . . . s-say . . . but just . . . leave me!"

The Marquis gave a deep sigh.

He took his arm from her and sat up on the side of the bed.

As he looked at Ursa he thought it was impossible for any woman to look so lovely and at the same time so pitiful.

There were tears on her cheeks, and now her eyes were pleading with him.

She was beseeching him in a way to which he could not put a name.

He got to his feet.

"I will leave you because you ask me to," he said, "but I do not think I have ever in the whole of my life been so disappointed, or felt so frustrated."

"I . . . I am . . . s-sorry," Ursa managed to whisper.

The Marquis stood for a moment, just looking down at her.

Then he turned and went back the way he had come.

Going through the communicating-door, he shut it quietly behind him.

Ursa was very still.

Then she turned, and burying her face in the pillow, burst into tears.

chapter six

URSA cried for a long time.

Then she blew out the candles and told herself she must go to sleep.

It was impossible, however, not to keep thinking of how wonderful the Marquis's kiss has been.

But she knew it was something she would never have again.

Now she must persuade the Dowager to go back to Brackley Park tomorrow.

'I will tell her,' she thought, 'that Arthur will be annoyed if I am not there when he returns.'

At the same time, every nerve in her body screamed at the idea of leaving Charnwood Court and the Marquis.

"I love . . . him! I . . . love . . . him!" she told herself in the darkness.

The tears flooded into her eyes.

Again she knew she must go to sleep, since otherwise she would not look herself in the morning.

She tried to imagine what she would do, or what she would say, when she saw the Marquis again.

She had a feeling he would not refer to what had occurred.

He would behave as if he were no longer interested in her.

'And that is the truth,' she thought. 'Because I have . . . refused to do what . . . Penelope would have . . . done, he will have no further . . . use for . . . me.'

It was difficult not to start crying all over again.

With a tremendous effort at self-control, she shut her eyes and said her prayers.

She prayed frantically that the Marquis would not hate her and that he would be happy.

'He will forget me,' she thought, 'but I will . . . never . . . never . . . forget him.'

She must have eventually fallen asleep, because she was suddenly aware that the door had opened and somebody had come into the room.

She opened her eyes.

To her astonishment, she saw a woman standing by the bed wearing dark glasses.

Before she could realise she was not dreaming, and it was actually happening, a sharp voice said:

"Wake up! Wake up, Ursa!"

"Penelope!"

The word came from between Ursa's lips in a gasp.

"Yes, it is me," Penelope said. "Now, hurry! You have to leave at once!"

"But . . . why? What has . . . happened?" Ursa asked in bewilderment.

"Arthur is already on his way home," Penelope said in a low voice, "and when he finds I am not at Brackley Park, he will come here."

As she spoke, she took off the dark glasses she was wearing and unfastened the chiffon scarf which she wore over her hat.

It tied under her chin in a large bow, making her, with the dark glasses, quite unrecognisable.

"Undo my gown!" Penelope ordered. "And put it on."

"I . . . I do not . . . understand what is . . . happening," Ursa said.

She was finding it difficult to think clearly, and it was as if her head were full of cotton-wool.

"Oh, do not be so stupid!" Penelope snapped. "All you have to do is to put on my clothes, get into the carriage that is waiting at the front-door for you, and be driven home."

Ursa did not speak, and Penelope went on:

"I cannot imagine why you came here in the first place, and I am really very angry about it!"

"I could not avoid it," Ursa explained. "The Marquis asked his Grandmother to help him and I . . . helped him too."

"What do you mean—you helped him?" Penelope asked.

She had taken off her gown.

Now she was removing the voluminous lace-edged petticoat which went under it.

"I am . . . afraid you will be . . . upset . . . when you hear what has . . . h-happened," Ursa said hesitatingly.

Penelope stood still.

"What has happened?" she asked.

Ursa for a moment found it difficult to speak.

Then she said almost incoherently:

"The Marquis had a ... very important Greek gentleman coming to ... see him ... who wanted ... him to ... marry his ... daughter."

"What has that to do with you?" Penelope enquired.

"To ... save him from ... a wife he does ... not want ... I agreed to pretend to ... be myself ... and he told ... the Greek he was ... engaged to me."

Penelope stared at her sister as if she could not believe what she was hearing.

"So you see," Ursa went on, "here at ... Charnwood Court I am ... supposed to be ... Miss Ursa Hollington ... and only the ... Marquis and his ... Grandmother think ... that I am ... really you."

"I have never heard of anything so muddleheaded in the whole of my life!" Penelope said furiously. "How could you become involved in anything so ridiculous, when you were supposed to be me?"

"Lady Brackley had ... no idea that the ... Marquis was coming to ... see her ... and as she is so ... fond of him ... of course she ... wanted to ... help him."

"So you are now here as yourself," Penelope said slowly, as if she were trying to understand.

"Yes ... that is ... right," Ursa said, "but the Greek visitors leave ... early this morning ... so I will ... not see them ... again."

"You mean *I* will not see them," Penelope corrected her sister, "and my mother-in-law will not be able to see any difference."

"B-but . . . suppose the . . . Marquis does?" Ursa asked.

A faint smile appeared on Penelope's lips.

"I have heard a great deal about Guy Charn," she said. "In fact, I am looking forward to meeting him."

"But . . . suppose he . . . realises you are not . . . me?"

"Do not worry about the Marquis," Penelope said in a confident tone. "I will deal with him! 'Birds of a feather flock together!' "

Ursa recalled what had happened last night.

If Penelope had been in her place, she would not have sent the Marquis away.

At the thought of it she felt as if a dagger had been stabbed into her heart.

Then, because there was nothing else she could do, she began to dress.

She put on the lace-edged petticoat and over it the extremely elaborate travelling-gown which Penelope had been wearing.

Penelope had already put on the nightgown which Ursa had been wearing.

She was loosening her hair so that it fell over her shoulders.

It was not as long as her sister's.

Yet she certainly looked very attractive as she looked at herself in the mirror.

Then she glanced at the clock.

As she did so, Ursa looked at it too and saw that the hands had not yet reached six o'clock.

She knew there would be no-one about except for a few of the servants.

If they had seen a lady wearing dark spectacles coming in, they would not be surprised to see her leaving.

Almost as if she had asked the question, Penelope said:

"I told the footman at the door that I was calling to see you with very important news which could not wait. But there was no need to disturb the rest of the household."

"That was clever of you," Ursa said.

"But there is nothing clever about the mess you have made of everything!" Penelope retorted sharply.

She had difficulty trying to button up Ursa's gown at the back herself.

Then she watched while her sister put on the very elaborate feather-trimmed hat she had been wearing.

The chiffon veil was of pale green, the colour of the gown.

It made Ursa's skin look very white and translucent, but it completed her disguise.

As she looked for her hand-bag, Penelope said:

"I suppose you had better take mine. There is some money in it, and you should tip the coachman."

"Is he your coachman?" Ursa asked, thinking perhaps he might reveal something to Arthur Brackley.

"No, of course not!" Penelope replied. "He belongs to Lord Vernon Winter. He has been in his service for a long time and is very discreet."

Ursa thought this at least was a relief.

At the same time, she could not help asking:

"How did you find out that Arthur is on his way to Brackley Park?"

"He is trying to catch me out!" Penelope explained. "It was stupid of me not to realise that was what he was doing but, if he has his spies, I have mine! I intended him to find his loving wife waiting for him with his Mother, but of course you had to go and mess everything up!"

"It was . . . not my fault . . . it really was . . . not!" Ursa protested.

Even as she spoke she knew that was not true.

It was she who had thought of the scheme to help the Marquis, she who had agreed to play the part of his "fiancée."

Before her sister could speak, she said:

"I am . . . sorry, Penelope . . . I am very . . . very sorry if I have . . . upset you."

"Fortunately I have brains enough to get out of this pickle," Penelope said. "Now, for goodness' sake, leave and do not speak to anybody until you are home!"

"N-no . . . of course . . . not," Ursa agreed.

She did not ask her sister if she was going to see her again, knowing what the answer would be.

As she moved towards the door, Penelope got into bed.

"At least this is comfortable," she said, "and actually, I am very tired with all this rushing about."

She sank back against the pillows.

"Oh, Ursa, do get on with it!" she groaned. "Why are you standing there, gaping? Go home, and stay home! And another time try not to alter my plans."

"I . . . I am sorry, Penelope," Ursa said again humbly.

"Now that I am here," Penelope said, "I am delighted to be able to see Charnwood Court, and, of course, meet its owner!"

She spoke in a soft, seductive voice.

Without another word, Ursa opened the door.

Outside in the corridor she could hear the servants moving about in the hall.

It was with the greatest difficulty that she forced herself to walk slowly and with dignity down the stairs.

A footman in his shirt-sleeves who was brushing a rug hastily opened the front-door for her.

At the bottom of the steps she could see a smart closed carriage drawn by four horses.

There was a coachman, and a footman on the box.

She stepped into it and as the door was shut the horses moved off.

She had a last glimpse of the house before they turned towards the bridge over the lake.

The swans were gliding smoothly over the still water.

Ursa knew, although she could not see it, that the Marquis's flag was flying over the centre tower.

He would be asleep in the Master bed-room in which generations of his ancestors had slept.

"Will he guess," she wondered, "that Penelope is not me?"

She could see again the little smile on her sister's lips and the glint of interest in her eyes as she had said:

" 'Birds of a feather flock together.' "

Ursa clenched her fingers together so tightly that they hurt.

"Now he will be with Penelope," she told herself, "and even if he knows she is not me, he will certainly not miss me!"

She wanted to cry, but she forced herself to keep back the tears.

As they passed through the great ornamental gates with the lodges on each side of them, she took off her dark spectacles.

She wanted to see for the last time the pretty thatched cottages with their flower-filled gardens.

Then the wall which surrounded the Marquis's Estate was left behind and she knew the drama was over.

Like "Cinderella," she was going back into obscurity and the Marquis would never think of her again.

"I love ... him! I ... love ... him!" she whispered.

The carriage wheels seemed to be repeating the words over and over again.

But they carried her further and further away from him.

*   *   *

The horses were travelling swiftly.

It did not take as long as Ursa had expected to reach her home.

As they drove down the small drive she felt as if she had been away for years.

Surprisingly, everything looked the same as it had when she left.

So much had happened in the short time she had been away.

She knew that she herself was different from the nervous girl who had left to take part in her sister's charade.

'I have fallen in love and I have been . . . kissed,' Ursa thought, 'so I suppose in some ways I have . . . grown up.'

Because her Father had always taught her to analyse her thoughts and feelings, she knew she was different.

However hard she might try, she could never step back, alter, or forget what had happened.

At the sound of the carriage wheels, old Dawson came hurrying to the door.

"You're back, Miss Ursa!" he exclaimed. "An' it's glad we are to see you! It don't seem th' same when you're not here."

"Thank you, Dawson," Ursa said.

She turned and pressed the money that was in Penelope's bag into the hand of the footman who had opened the carriage door for her.

Now, as she was talking to Dawson, the coachman turned the horses, and they were moving away.

Dawson looked astonished and asked in surprise:

"B'aint they stopping for a cup of tea, Miss Ursa?"

"No, Dawson," she answered. "They are in a hurry to go back to where they came from."

"An' what's happened to your luggage?" he asked.

"It is arriving later," Ursa explained.

It was, in fact, the first time she had thought about it.

Now she realised that Penelope had arrived with nothing and would therefore want what she had given Ursa to take with her, besides, of course, being glad to have Marie looking after her again.

Aloud Ursa said:

"I will go upstairs and change, Dawson."

"Yes, indeed, Miss Ursa," Dawson agreed. "You look real smart, an' it'd be a pity to spoil that pretty gown."

She had started up the stairs, when Dawson gave a cry.

"Oh, Miss Ursa, I nearly forgot . . ."

"What is it?" she asked, stopping to turn on the stairs.

"There be a letter here for you. It comes about an hour ago. Very urgent I was told it were."

"A letter?" Ursa said. "I wonder who it is from?"

Because she knew it hurt Dawson's arthritic legs to climb the stairs, she ran down them again.

He handed her the letter which was lying on one of the side-tables in the hall.

One glance at it told Ursa it was from her Father.

"Oh, it is from Papa, Dawson!" she exclaimed. "How lovely! I do hope he is coming home soon."

"I hopes so too, Miss Ursa," Dawson agreed.

"It be lonely here for you when the Master's ain't wi' us."

Ursa did not answer because she was climbing the stairs again.

When she reached her bed-room she pulled off her hat and threw it with the gloves and bag onto the bed.

She sat down at the dressing-table and opened the letter.

She suspected, as it had arrived so quickly after he had gone away, that he had sent it through the Dutch Embassy.

This was something he had often done in the past.

His distinctive hand-writing was very familiar.

As she drew out the sheets of writing-paper she felt a warmth within her.

Even hearing from him made it seem as if he was near her.

Slowly, so as not to miss a word, she read:

"My dearest beloved Daughter:

I know this will come as a great surprise, but by the time you receive this I will be married. I have known Theresa van Bergen for many years because, as I am sure you will remember, I have been in constant touch with her husband when we have exchanged books and manuscripts.

Theresa, who is English, was very much younger than her husband, and when he died nine months ago, I hoped and prayed that one day she might turn to me for comfort.

When she did so, I was able to reveal that I loved her.

Now we can be together and, as she is as interested in my work as I am, it should be a very advantageous and happy companionship.

I am confident, my dearest Ursa, that when you meet Theresa you will love her as I do, and I have told her so much about you that she says she feels as if she knows and loves you already.

I know you will understand that having just married, we want to spend some time alone together before we come back to England.

We are going first to Rome, where there are some manuscripts we both want to see, then down to the South of Italy.

I have put two addresses at the end of this letter where you can write to me, and I hope, my dearest, you will not feel that the happiness we have known together has come to an end, but believe as I do that it will be increased through having Theresa with us.

Take care of yourself, and send me your good wishes, because I shall be waiting to receive them.

> *I remain,*
> *Your affectionate and loving Father,*
> *Matthew Hollington."*

Ursa read the letter, and she could not believe what it contained.

It had never crossed her mind that her Father would marry again.

She had never imagined that he could love another woman after he had lost her Mother.

They had always seemed so utterly and completely devoted to each other.

It seemed almost sacrilege that he should not remain faithful to her memory.

Then, as she thought it over, Ursa told herself that she was being very childish.

Her Father was still a comparatively young man, not yet fifty, and extremely active both physically and mentally.

He had always been absorbed in his work and seemed quite content to have her as his companion.

It had never occurred to her that he might need a more mature woman to keep him happy.

"How could I have been so stupid as to think that all Papa wanted was books and documents, which could not breathe or speak?" she asked herself.

He himself had so much personality that it was not surprising he attracted women.

If he had fallen in love with Theresa, then, of course, Theresa had fallen in love with him.

As she thought of it, she calculated that her Father was ten or fifteen years younger than his friend, van Bergen.

Looking back, she could remember how her Father had said he had enjoyed staying with the van Bergens.

He had added that his hostess had been very attentive to him, and was also very lovely.

"How can I have been so stupid as not to realise after Mama died that Papa would be lonely?" Ursa asked herself. "I am too young to be a real companion to him."

She said the last words bitterly.

Getting up from the dressing-table, she walked to the window.

She looked out into the garden that seemed brilliant with flowers.

The small fountain was throwing its water up into the sky.

She had always been happy in her home.

Now she knew she would have to leave it.

Her Father might protest, but what woman, and a Bride, would not want to be alone with the man she loved?

"Where can . . . I go? What shall . . . I do?" Ursa asked herself.

Once again the tears were back in her eyes.

She changed her clothes and went out into the garden.

For the first time, the beauty of it failed to enrapture her.

Instead of seeing the flowers and hearing the song of the birds, she could think only of Charnwood.

By now the Greeks would have left and Penelope would be downstairs.

She wondered if the Marquis would instantly be aware of the change.

Perhaps, after last night, he would avoid looking at her.

He might even go riding by himself, she thought, or perhaps make some excuse to his Grandmother and the girls who had rebuffed him to take them straight back to Brackley Park.

That, she confessed to herself, was what she really wanted him to do.

She knew it was because she was jealous.

She was jealous of Penelope, with her beauty and her seductive ways, surrendering herself to the Marquis.

He would, of course, quite easily get from Penelope what she had refused to give him.

As she thought about it, Ursa felt as if a hundred voices were jeering and laughing at her.

"You loved him, and he loved you! What more could you want?"

It was then, as she sat down on the seat in front of the fountain, that Ursa told herself that what the Marquis felt for her was not love.

It was not the love she had thought about, dreamed of, and which had inspired the poems she had read.

It was not something so beautiful that it seemed a part of her prayers.

The love she wanted was what her Father and Mother had had for each other.

It was the love for which men had fought and died since the beginning of civilisation.

It was the love that was very human, and yet a part of God.

As she had grown older her longing for it had seemed to creep into her dreams.

She had thought of it when she looked up at the stars.

She had thought in her head that perhaps one day they would send her the love for which she was seeking.

"I found it only to lose it again," she murmured bitterly.

As she spoke, she looked at the fountain.

It was almost as if she saw the Marquis's handsome face in the irridescent water which rose and fell in the sunlight.

Because the agony of it was unbearable, she rose and walked back into the house.

As she did so, she knew that whenever she saw anything beautiful in the future, or heard music, or felt it within herself, she would think of the Marquis.

The Marquis—who was as far out of reach as the stars, amongst which she had once sought love.

chapter seven

THE Marquis saw off his Greek guests after breakfast.

Alexis Orestes left affably, telling the Marquis how much he was looking forward to entertaining him and his wife in Athens.

As they drove down the drive the Marquis gave a sigh of relief, then walked towards the stables.

He chose his favourite stallion and set off alone.

At first he galloped very fast, then he moved more slowly.

He had been unable to sleep after leaving Ursa's bed-room.

He had lain awake, finding it impossible to believe that for the first time in his life he had been refused by a beautiful woman.

He had learnt of Penelope's beauty and her frequent love-affairs almost as soon as he had set foot on English soil.

She was gossiped about at every party to which he was invited.

He could not help feeling sorry for Arthur Brackley.

At the same time, as he grew up, he realised that Arthur was old, even for his age, and rather ponderous.

When he learned that Arthur Brackley had married again, he had been abroad.

He had received the news in a letter from his Grandmother.

It seemed to him odd that Arthur should have married anybody described as so young and beautiful.

When later he learnt that Arthur's new wife was being unfaithful to him, he was not really surprised.

He was mature enough to recognise that there had been a revolution in the behaviour of married women.

Those who were both beautiful and of social importance were ready to take lover after lover.

This was socially acceptable as long as their husbands were either unaware of it or else ignored it.

The Marquis thought now that from the moment he had met Penelope at his Grandmother's house he had found her very different from what he had expected.

There was an air of innocence about her.

He assumed it was an act, but such a clever one that it was difficult not to be deceived by it.

Because she had not only attracted him, but also intrigued and puzzled him, he had gone to her bed-room.

He had expected to learn the secret of how, with such a reputation, she managed to look so "untouched," what he could describe to himself only as "spiritual."

He had enjoyed the intelligent and interesting conversations they had had.

But she had never attempted to flirt with him as most other women did.

He found himself talking to her in the same way that he might have done with one of his men-friends.

Yet—she had refused him!

She had sent him away, and he could only ask why he had been a failure.

And why had she been so frightened?

He could still hear the fear in her voice.

There was no doubt that the tears which had filled her eyes were real.

"Why? Why?" he asked.

It was a puzzle he could not unravel.

He rode on, unaware of where he was going or what he was doing.

He could see only two blue eyes filled with tears, and a childlike voice telling him he was frightening her.

"I do not understand!" he muttered as he turned for home. "I just—do not understand!"

It was getting near luncheontime as he rode into the stables.

His Chief Groom, who had obviously been looking out for him, came hurrying to take hold of the stallion's bridle.

"Did ye 'ave a good ride, M'Lord?" he asked.

"Yes—thank you," the Marquis replied in a dull voice.

He dismounted heavily.

Trying to think of something other than his personal problems, he said:

"Oh, by the way, Gavin, I think we should try to get another team at least as good as the one we have already."

He saw a light come into his Chief Groom's eyes, and he went on:

"I was delighted with their performance when I drove them over to Brackley, but for longer journeys we must have a change."

"Oi agrees with ye, M'Lord," Gavin replied, "and let's 'ope we'll find summat as good as they chestnuts Oi spied standin' outside th' front-door this marnin'."

"Chestnuts?" the Marquis enquired.

"Aye, M'Lord, an' nought between 'em! The best four chestnuts Oi've seen in a long time."

He saw the Marquis was interested, and he went on:

"Oi says t' th' coachman, as Oi've met afore:

" 'Ow fast does they go?'

" 'They flies like swallows,' he answers, 'their feet never touches t'ground.' "

The Marquis smiled.

"They sound good, and it is a pity we have nothing like them."

"They was sold only a month since," Gavin said, "an' 'Is Lordship got a bargain."

"His Lordship?" the Marquis exclaimed, then asked:

"Whom do they belong to?"

"Lord Vernon Winter, M'Lord."

The Marquis was still. Then he asked:

"And they were here this morning?"

"Aye, M'Lord, 'bout six o'clock, it were."

The Marquis longed to ask more questions, but thought it would be a mistake.

As he walked towards the house, he was thinking that it was very strange.

Why should Vernon Winter, whom he knew well, be calling so early?

Why had he not been informed of it?

Vernon Winter had been at Eton with him, then at Oxford until he had been sent down.

He had stayed out all night with a woman who was appearing at the local Theatre.

Even when he was in India, the Earl had continued to hear about Lord Vernon Winter's love-affairs.

Just before he left for home there had been talk about a duel in which Vernon had been involved.

It had taken place in Green Park.

Somewhat unfairly, the husband who had challenged him because of his behaviour towards his wife had been injured.

Vernon, however, had escaped scot-free.

If Vernon had come to Charnwood Court, then it could have been only to see Penelope.

But why so early in the morning?

And why had he not been told of His Lordship's visit?

The Marquis strode into the hall.

The Butler was there as well as two footmen.

When the Marquis had handed his hat, whip, and gloves to him, he asked:

"Who was on duty first thing this morning?"

"That was Henry, M'Lord," the Butler replied.

He indicated, as he spoke, one of the footmen.

"I understand," the Marquis said, "we had an early caller this morning—in fact, six o'clock I believe it was."

"Yes, M'Lord," Henry answered. "I'd just come on duty."

"Who was it?" the Marquis enquired.

"T'were a lady, M'Lord."

"Did she give her name?"

"No, M'Lord. Her said her had to see th' young lady as come 'ere with Yer Lordship's Grandmother, an' t' were a matter o' urgency. Then her went upstairs."

The Marquis thought for a moment before he asked:

"How long was she here?"

" 'Bout fifteen t' twenty minutes, M'Lord."

"Then she left?"

"Her did, M'Lord."

"Did you in fact recognise her?"

"Her were wearing dark spectacles, M'Lord, very dark, they be."

"She was still wearing them when she left?"

"Her was, M'Lord."

The Marquis did not say any more.

He was thinking as he walked away that now he knew what had happened.

The answer to the puzzle came to him like a light in the darkness.

He went upstairs and changed from his riding-clothes.

As he did so, he was certain that his acute brain had the answer to everything that had perplexed him.

As he went downstairs there was an alert look about him which those who knew him well would have recognised.

He entered the Drawing-Room.

He saw at the end of it, sitting in her favourite chair by the fireplace, was his Grandmother.

On a sofa opposite her was a woman with fair hair.

As he walked towards them she turned her head.

He knew immediately that he was seeing Penelope Brackley for the first time.

She was beautiful, there was no denying that, but in a very different way from her sister.

He kissed his Grandmother, then said to the woman sitting opposite her:

"Good-morning! I trust you slept well."

"But of course!" Penelope answered. "It is so comfortable and luxurious in your beautiful house!"

She looked at him, as she spoke, with an expression with which the Marquis was very familiar.

He had seen it on so many women's faces.

It was deliberately provocative, with an invitation in their eyes and the movement of their lips.

He was well aware that Ursa had never looked at him like that.

Nevertheless Penelope's voice was indeed very similar to her sister's.

The Marquis could understand how his Grandmother had been deceived.

He glanced at the clock, thinking it was time for luncheon.

At that moment the door opened and the Butler announced:

"Lord Brackley, M'Lord!"

Arthur Brackley walked in, and Penelope gave an excited cry.

"Arthur! Arthur!" she exclaimed. "You are back! How wonderful!"

She ran across the room and flung herself against him.

Putting her arms round his neck, she drew his head down to hers.

The Marquis was aware it was an act, and a very good one.

"I went to the Park," Arthur was saying, "and found you had come here. I cannot imagine why."

"That was my fault," the Dowager said, "and it is delightful to see you, dear Arthur."

"How are you, Mama?" Lord Brackley asked, bending to kiss her cheek.

Penelope was still clinging to him, her face lifted up to his.

"I have missed you, Darling," she said. "I cannot tell you how lonely it has been without you."

"I find that difficult to believe," Lord Brackley said ponderously.

He was looking at the Marquis as he spoke, who said:

"We will tell you all about it over luncheon."

Arthur Brackley drew a gold watch from his waist-coat pocket and said:

"It will have to be a quick meal. I have to leave for London as soon as possible, and take Penelope with me."

"I will have everything packed at once!" Penelope said eagerly. "It will be so wonderful to be back in London again, Darling, and with you."

The Marquis found it hard not to applaud what appeared to be a note of complete sincerity in her voice.

He was also impressed by the manner in which she moved sensuously a little closer to her husband.

To Lord Brackley he said:

"I will give orders so that you will not be delayed for longer than is necessary."

He went from the room.

A few minutes later the Butler announced that luncheon was served.

It was not yet two o'clock when, thanks to the Marquis's excellent organisation, Lord Brackley and his wife drove off in the carriage in which he had arrived.

As soon as they were out of sight, the Marquis's Chaise, drawn by his team of four, came round from the stables.

The Marquis was in the Drawing-Room with his Grandmother.

"There is something I want to ask you, Grandmama," he said.

"What is it?" she enquired.

"Where does Matthew Hollington live?"

There was a smile on the Dowager's lips as she replied:

"In a little village called Letty Green. It is not far from here if you go direct and not the way we came via Brackley Park."

"Thank you," the Marquis said.

He was just about to kiss his Grandmother good-bye, when she asked:

"I suppose you are going to find Ursa?"

The Marquis was still.

"So you knew?" he questioned.

"I suspected from the first," the Dowager admitted, "and then, when Penelope arrived this morning, I was absolutely sure!"

The Marquis did not say anything, and she went on:

"To be honest, my Dearest, I never cared for Penelope. I always thought she might be beautiful outside, which, of course, I could not see, but her beauty does not go very deep. In fact, I am certain she is entirely superficial."

"And Ursa?"

The Dowager smiled.

"She is very different. There is something exquisitely lovely about her which I felt the moment she arrived."

Her voice softened as she went on:

"When I heard her speaking Greek to your friends, and reading Greek poetry to me, not just with her eyes, but with her heart, I knew she was everything a 'nymph of the sea' should be."

The Marquis drew in his breath.

Then he bent down and kissed his Grandmother.

"Thank you, Grandmama," he said. "Please stay

here for as long as you like, and I know everyone will look after you."

"I love being here," the Dowager said, "and when you do come back, bring Ursa with you."

The Marquis did not answer.

He merely went from the room.

The Dowager sat back with a smile on her lips, praying that what she wanted would come true.

* * *

The Marquis drove his team faster than he had ever driven them before.

He remembered the countryside well and he therefore had no difficulty in finding Letty Green.

The first person he asked on entering the village directed him to the house where Matthew Hollington lived.

The Marquis drew up his team with a flourish just after four o'clock.

He handed the reins to his groom, getting down, and walked up to the front-door.

It was open, and without ringing the bell the Marquis walked inside.

There was a door at the end of the hall which was open, and he could see there was nobody inside.

As if his instinct were guiding him, he walked down a passage and opened a door at the end of it.

He saw as he entered that the walls were lined with books.

He felt this was the most likely place he would find Ursa.

He was not mistaken, although at first glance the room was empty.

Then he saw her.

She was lying on a sofa, her head on a cushion, fast asleep.

The Marquis stood looking down at her, thinking it was impossible for anyone to look more lovely.

At the same time, she was young, unspoiled, and, as he now knew, untouched.

Slowly he moved towards the sofa, then went down on his knees beside her.

Her eye-lashes, he saw, were still wet with tears.

Unable to prevent himself, he bent forward and gently his lips touched her.

He was aware of the little quiver that went through her.

Without opening her eyes she whispered:

"I . . . love . . . you . . . I . . . love . . . you!"

"That is what I want to hear, my Darling," the Marquis answered.

His voice roused her, and she looked up at him in bewilderment.

"I . . . I was . . . dreaming," she said, "but . . . you are . . . real."

"I am very real," the Marquis answered, "and I am here to prove it."

He bent forward, and now his lips were more demanding.

It was a long kiss, and to Ursa it was as if the heavens had opened and the stars were falling down.

She could feel them on her breast and moving through her body.

She could not think.

All she knew was that the Marquis was there and there was nothing in the world but him.

Only when he raised his head did she manage to say a little incoherently:

"Why . . . why are you . . . h-here? . . . h-how did you . . . f-find . . . me?"

"How could you have gone away without letting me know?" he asked. "Do you really think I could lose you?"

"B-but . . . Penelope . . ." Ursa stammered.

"Your sister has gone back to London with her husband," the Marquis said, "and now there need be no more pretence, no more lies."

He saw the colour come into Ursa's cheeks, and her eyes looked shy.

"I . . . I am . . . s-sorry," she said. "I was . . . pretending . . . at first to . . . h-help . . . Penelope—"

"And then to help me!" the Marquis finished. "Now we can just be ourselves. What I want to know, my lovely one, is how soon you will marry me?"

Ursa's eyes opened wide.

"M-marry . . . you? You are . . . asking me to . . . marry . . . you?" she whispered. "But . . . how can I . . . after I have . . . pretended . . . to be . . . Penelope . . . and she . . . will be . . . very . . . angry."

"I am not concerned with your sister's feelings," the Marquis said. "I think, my Darling, that in all this mix-up and pretence we have found something more important than anything else."

His lips were very near to hers as he said softly:

"It is called Love, the real love for which I have been seeking all my life."

Ursa gave a little gasp.

"I love you . . . I love you . . . with all my

heart . . . and soul!" she said. "B-but how . . . can I . . . marry you? What would your . . . Grandmother . . . say?"

"My Grandmother will be delighted!" the Marquis replied. "It was she who told me where you live, and also that she knew you were not Penelope from the very first."

"H-how could . . . she have . . . known that?" Ursa questioned in dismay.

"Because you are so very different in every way from your sister," the Marquis said, "and you must forgive me, my darling one, for last night."

Almost as if she had forgotten what had happened the previous night, Ursa gave a little gasp.

Then she was blushing and hiding her face in the Marquis's shoulder.

He held her very close to him.

"You are so very different from what I expected," he said, "but my mind had been poisoned by the gossip I had heard about you, or, rather, your sister, and because I wanted you more than I have ever wanted anyone before, I was foolish enough to frighten you."

"I . . . I have been . . . crying," Ursa whispered, "because I . . . sent . . . you away . . . and I thought that . . . now I would . . . never see . . . you again . . . and it was a . . . stupid thing to . . . have done."

"It was the right thing to do," the Marquis said, "and I cannot imagine you ever doing anything wrong."

Then he asked in a different tone of voice:

"How many men have kissed you?"

"No . . . no-one except . . . y-you," Ursa replied.

"That is what I thought," the Marquis said as he smiled, "and, my Darling, no-one else ever will, and I will kill any man who tries!"

"I . . . would never let . . . another man . . . touch me," Ursa said, "when I love . . . you. I was so . . . lonely and unhappy . . . when I came home . . . I was sure you . . . hated . . . me."

"I was bewildered by you," the Marquis admitted. "Why did you say you were lonely when you came home?"

Ursa hesitated for a moment and then she handed him her Father's letter.

The Marquis read it and remarked:

"Well, that certainly makes things easier for us."

She looked at him in surprise, and he said:

"I have been waiting to ask you, how soon will you marry me?"

Ursa gave a little gasp.

"Have you . . . really asked . . . me to marry . . . you?"

"I will put it a little clearer," the Marquis said, smiling. "I want to marry you, I intend to marry you, and you are the only person I have ever proposed to in the whole of my life."

Ursa clasped her hands together.

It sounded too wonderful, but at the same time she hesitated.

"What is worrying you?" the Marquis asked gently.

In a very small voice she answered:

"You . . . know your . . . reputation of being . . . very dashing and . . . making love to . . . lots of sophisticated and . . . exciting women . . . in London."

The Marquis did not say anything.

After a moment Ursa went on in a voice that could hardly be heard:

"How . . . could I . . . compete with . . . that?"

The Marquis put his arms around her and said:

"Now, listen to me, my Darling, I suppose I expected this question to come up sooner or later as far as you and I are concerned. Although, as I have said, you intrigue and excite me until it is difficult for me to think straight."

"But you . . . have to," Ursa insisted. "Loving you is . . . one thing . . . but being . . . married . . ."

She gave a little shiver.

"If I . . . bored you . . . and you . . . left me . . . there would be . . . nothing for . . . me to do . . . but wish . . . to die."

The Marquis pulled her closer to him.

"You are not going to die. We are going to live together and be supremely and utterly happy so that everyone will be astonished."

"How can . . . you be . . . sure?" Ursa asked.

"I will tell you exactly," the Marquis said. "I am asking you to marry me, my Precious, because you are the most attractive, the most beautiful, and quite the most adorable woman I have ever met."

He paused before he said in a very different tone of voice:

"I am also asking you to be something else in my life, something which no other woman could be."

Ursa looked at him in astonishment.

"What is . . . that?" she asked.

"I think the right word," the Marquis said slowly, "is my Partner."

"Your Partner?" Ursa repeated. "I do not . . . understand."

"Now let me think it out clearly," the Marquis said. "When you were pretending to be your sister, you were so clever and so diplomatic with Mr. Orestes that I told myself that was exactly the sort of woman I wanted in my life to help me with all the things I am doing."

He gave a little laugh before he said:

"I must admit I have never thought of having a woman before, but I have often wished I had someone to help me and someone to discuss things with and with whom I could be quite certain my secrets were safe."

"I still do . . . not . . . understand," Ursa murmured.

"As I was saying," the Marquis answered, "you were marvellous with Orestes, and he genuinely wanted you to come with me to Greece. I am quite certain that at the back of his crafty mind he thought you would be an asset in what I was doing for them with their Battleships."

"You . . . cannot mean . . . that," Ursa said.

"I do mean it," he answered. "Since then I have talked to you about a great number of things and you have astounded me with your intelligent questions and also your knowledge of foreign affairs, which I certainly never expected to find in your sister."

"How . . . could I . . . tell you," Ursa asked, "that I had . . . travelled to many . . . strange places . . .

with Papa and met so many ... interesting people."

"I have a feeling," the Marquis said, "that you speak quite a lot of foreign languages."

"Quite a number," Ursa admitted.

"That is another thing where I want your help. My French is good, my Italian passable, and that is all."

"You know I ... will help you ... if I can," Ursa answered.

"That is what you are going to do," he said firmly. "My Partner, who is also my lovely wife, will have to do her share of the business whether it concerns Greece, other parts of the world, or in making Charnwood as perfect as I want it to be."

"Now you are ... frightening me," Ursa said. "How could I ... possibly do all ... those things?"

"Very easily," the Marquis answered. "And I promise you I shall work you very hard."

Ursa looked up at him.

There was a pleading look in her eyes which he thought was very touching.

"Promise me ... you are ... telling me ... the truth," she said, "and not just ... saying it because ... you know it will ... make me ... happy."

"I am saying it because I mean every word and I want you desperately," the Marquis said. "You have already inspired me with ideas of great things I might do in the future."

Ursa made a little sound of delight, and he went on:

"If you are not there to prod me along and at

the same time make me lift my eyes to the stars, I might easily fail."

Ursa laughed.

"Now you are being modest. You know you are . . . brilliant and I have . . . a feeling you will . . . never fail in . . . anything you . . . undertake."

"There is one thing I am not going to fail at," the Marquis said, "and that is in marrying you. Now, tell me, my Darling, how soon will you marry me?"

Ursa turned her face against his shoulder.

"You know . . . so little . . . about me," she whispered, "only the . . . pretend . . . me."

"I have adored the pretend you," the Marquis said, "and I am quite certain I shall adore the real you when I get to know her. We cannot waste time."

"There is not . . . really so much . . . hurry," Ursa said tentatively.

"There is," the Marquis said. "For one thing, I am not going to have you living alone here now that your Father is away and not coming back for a long time. So I am taking you back to Charnwood, and the sooner we are married, the easier it will be."

"Easier!" Ursa questioned.

"Certainly very much easier for me," he said, "than lying awake, wanting you, loving you, and knowing that I have to put a ring on your finger before I come into your bed-room."

Ursa blushed.

He thought it was something he had seen happen to very few women of his acquaintance.

"Suppose," she said, "when you do . . . marry

me I . . . cannot do . . . everything you . . . want and you . . . find you have been too . . . hasty in . . . making up . . . your mind."

The Marquis laughed.

"I made up my mind a long time ago, it seems to me, although I suppose it was not very long in days and hours. You are everything a man desires in a woman, and as you are unique and the only woman in the world for me, I am not going to risk losing you."

His arms tightened as he said:

"You are mine, Ursa, mine completely already. Our brains work together, we know each other's thoughts, and all we have to do now is to get married without causing any comment."

"The servants at Charnwood," Ursa murmured, "must be aware that Penelope took my place."

"The senior servants will know that," the Marquis said, "but as they have been with my family for so long, they will not talk to outsiders. If they were shocked at your sister's behaviour, that does not affect you. You came as Ursa and as Ursa you will return."

He kissed her forehead before he added:

"I know that as my wife they will welcome you with open arms, as will my relatives when they know about it."

"Have you . . . a great . . . number of . . . them?" Ursa asked nervously.

"Too many," the Marquis replied. "But I am not going to inflict them upon you until we have had a long honeymoon and, of course, visited Greece, where you will have to help me with my plans."

Ursa did not speak, and after a moment he said:

"Well, now that that is settled, I will send my Secretary to London tomorrow to get a Special Licence. We will be married in the Chapel with only my Grandmother present."

"That is just the sort of wedding I would like," Ursa cried. "But I am sure your friends will be very disappointed and expect you to have a big reception with hundreds of people with whom you must shake hands."

"Something I have always dreaded," the Marquis said. "If anything bores me, it is people who talk and talk about a wedding before it takes place and argue as to who are the most important members of the family."

"At least you will . . . not have to . . . worry about that," Ursa suggested.

"The only thing I want," the Marquis answered, "is for you to remember your wedding as one of the happiest moments of your life."

"It . . . all sounds . . . too wonderful to . . . be true," Ursa murmured.

"It will," the Marquis said firmly, "be very, very wonderful, my Darling, and something we shall always remember."

When he finished speaking, he kissed her.

He went on kissing her until they were both breathless.

Then he said in a rather unsteady tone:

"Get your hat and we will go back to Charnwood."

To his surprise, Ursa did not immediately move from his arms.

Instead, she said hesitatingly:

"I have . . . something to . . . ask . . . you."

"What is it," he enquired.

"You said you wanted to be . . . married . . . at once . . . but could you . . . please give . . . me time to get . . . just a few . . . new gowns."

The Marquis looked surprised, but she went on quickly.

"What you have seen me wearing up to now . . . is what I was lent by Penelope," Ursa said. "When she arrived she just gave me the dress she was wearing in which to leave. All the things I brought to Charnwood were left behind."

The Marquis laughed.

"I had forgotten," he said, "how important clothes are to a woman, and, of course, my Darling, you must have a trousseau even if we have to buy it very quickly and augment it at every place we stop at on our honeymoon."

"Do you mean . . . that?" Ursa asked. "I know it makes me feel a little better . . . but this is the first time you have . . . seen me as . . . a country-bumpkin and you might be very . . . disillusioned."

The Marquis looked down at her and thought, 'How could any woman look so lovely?'

He also actually preferred her without the artificial touching up which had been done to make her look like her sister.

Because there had been a number of smart, sophisticated women in his life, he understood exactly what Ursa was feeling.

He knew it was something which must not trouble her in the future.

"You shall have the most beautiful clothes from the best shops in Bond Street," he promised.

"Are we going to London?" Ursa exclaimed nervously.

"Certainly not," the Marquis replied. "But they will send their best gowns down for us to choose from and you can leave that to me. I will help you look as lovely as any Greek Goddess when she stepped down from Olympus."

Ursa laughed.

"I can hardly believe that. But doubtless Mr. Orestes will be very . . . flattered if we . . . tell him that is what I am . . . trying to do."

"I shall make certain," the Marquis said, "that Mr. Orestes keeps his conversation with you on Battleships and the improvements we are making to them."

Ursa gave a little laugh.

Then he said:

"I am serious, I assure you I will be a very jealous husband and make quite certain there is no other man in your life except me."

"You cannot . . . believe I would . . . want one?" Ursa asked. "How could I? No-one could be so clever or so . . . wonderful as . . . you."

"That is what I want you to believe," the Marquis said. "And now that we have settled that problem, have you any more?"

"No," Ursa said, "except I find it difficult to . . . believe this is really . . . happening."

The Marquis got off the sofa, and when Ursa did the same, he pulled her close to him.

"I love you," he said, "and it is difficult to think

of anything else. But we have to be very practical and sensible about this. I am sure we are right in thinking it would be a great mistake for anyone to know we are married until we are out of England and safely on our way to the Mediterranean."

"Are we . . . going straight . . . to Greece?" Ursa asked.

The Marquis shook his head.

"I am planning something very special in my mind, which I think, my Darling, will make you happy, but we will talk about it later. Now I want to get home, where Grandmama is waiting to tell you you are the answer to her prayers."

He kissed her again before she could speak, and then she left him to go upstairs to her bed-room.

chapter eight

THE Marquis looked around the room where they had been together.

He saw the books which belonged to her Father and thought if a woman could understand them, the more ordinary problems of everyday business should be easy.

"She is unique," he told himself. "I know that loving her is going to make my life very different in the future from what it has been in the past."

He could not help thinking that what he had done in India and in Greece seemed satisfactory.

Yet quite a lot of his life had been spent in pursuing beautiful women.

He had been aware since he had been at School and University that he was cleverer than most of his contemporaries.

He thought now that Ursa would inspire him to achieve more than even he expected in his wildest ambitions.

It did not seem possible that anyone so beautiful should also be so clever.

He knew instinctively that he was not mistaken and that their future was paved with gold.

When Ursa came downstairs she went first into the Kitchen and told the old couple that she was going to Charnwood Court.

"That'll be real nice for you, Miss Ursa," they said.

She also told them that her Father was married.

They were extremely surprised.

At the same time, they were not as nervous about having a new mistress as she was afraid they might have been.

"Papa will be returning here sometime," she said at length, "and so will I. I know you will look after everything for us and I will arrange to send you money every week."

"It sounds as if you too are going abroad, Miss Ursa," the old man-servant said.

"Well, I may," Ursa replied. "If you need anything, or anything goes wrong, then tell the Vicar. You know he will help you in any way he can."

"Nothing'll go wrong while we're in charge," the couple said.

A few minutes later Ursa drove away with the Marquis and they waved to her quite happily.

They did not resent her leaving as she was afraid they might have.

The Marquis had his magnificent team to drive.

Every time he stole a quick glance at Ursa he thought she looked more beautiful than the time before.

She was, in fact, feeling he was carrying her away from all the loneliness and unhappiness of which she had been so afraid.

He was taking her to a Paradise which she had imagined was only in her heart and thought would never actually be hers.

'I love . . . you, I love . . . you,' she wanted to say over and over again.

Because she was afraid that he might think it over-demonstrative, she sat only a little nearer to him.

Occasionally she put her hand on his knee.

As they were travelling so fast, they did not talk very much.

Finally Charnwood Court came in sight.

It looked even more like a Fairy Palace, Ursa thought, than the first time she had seen it.

'Is it really possible,' she asked herself as they drove under the old oak trees, 'that I am to be married to a fairy-tale Prince?'

He was in a way still as unreal as if he had stepped out of a picture book.

Because he knew what she was feeling, the Marquis did not say anything until the horses came to a standstill outside the front-door.

Then he said very softly:

"Welcome home, my Darling."

She smiled at him.

Then as the grooms came running from the stables, the footmen opened the door of the Chaise.

They stepped out to walk up the red carpet and in through the front-door.

"Is Her Ladyship downstairs?" the Marquis asked Hutton, who was waiting for them.

"Yes, My Lord. Her Ladyship is in the Drawing-Room."

Taking Ursa by the hand, the Marquis walked into the room.

As Ursa expected, the Dowager was sitting in the window with the evening sun shining on her white hair.

They were not announced, and only when they were halfway across the room did Lady Brackley say:

"Is that you, Guy?"

"It is, Grandmama, and I have brought Ursa back with me."

The Dowager rose to her feet and held out her arms.

"I am so glad, so very glad."

The Marquis kissed her and then Ursa did the same.

"You have something to tell me?" the Dowager enquired.

"We are to be married as quickly as possible, Grandmama," the Marquis replied.

"That is what I have prayed for. I know that Ursa is exactly the wife you should have."

Because she spoke with such sincerity, Ursa felt the tears come into her eyes.

"I never thought when I came . . . here that . . . this could . . . happen," she said.

"I know that, dear child," the Dowager said. "But as you told me, people who are blind have a perception that those who can see do not have. I knew from the moment you came here pretending to be your sister that you were very different from what she is."

She smiled and then said softly:

"Then I grew to love you and thought perhaps you were the person God had sent for my favourite and most beloved grandson."

"You were quite right, Grandmama," the Marquis said, "and now you must help us plan our wedding so that there is no talk, no scandal, and no-one need know anything about it until we are on our honeymoon."

"That should not be too difficult for three minds that think alike," the Dowager said as she smiled.

They had a delicious dinner, the Marquis making them laugh with stories of his adventures in India.

He persuaded Ursa to relate all the places she had been with her Father.

She told them of the unusual food she had enjoyed with different tribes in Africa, and other parts of the East.

When finally the Dowager went to bed, Ursa lingered in the Drawing-Room for a few minutes.

"Are you happy?" the Marquis asked.

"So happy, it is . . . impossible for me to put it . . . into . . . words," Ursa replied.

"Then tomorrow you must play the piano for me," he said.

It was something he had not mentioned until then.

"I want to listen to you, and it makes it easier not to keep kissing you as I want to."

"Easier?" Ursa asked rather surprised.

"I love you so overwhelmingly," the Marquis said, "that I do not want to frighten you as I did the other night, so I must wait until you are my wife to tell you how much I love you."

He knew as he spoke that Ursa did not really understand.

He was so thrilled by the fact that no other man had made love to her.

She had no idea how wildly and desperately he wanted her.

At the same time, her purity and innocence were what he had always desired in his wife.

He knew that no man could be more fortunate than he was in finding someone who was, as Ursa thought herself, another part of him.

Finally he took Ursa upstairs and kissed her gently before she went into her bed-room.

He walked to his own room, thanking God as he did so that she was so utterly and completely different from the women with whom he had had fiery affairs which had soon faded away.

It was difficult even after a short time to recall their faces and their charms.

As he got into bed he was thinking of how he would make Ursa's wedding so beautiful that they would both remember it for the rest of their lives.

To Ursa, every day was more like a fairy-tale.

The Marquis consulted his Grandmother and then said:

"I want to send a messenger to the best shops in Bond Street."

He wrote down exactly what he required, and also his housekeeper took Ursa's measurements.

The next day, what seemed to Ursa a mountain of clothes, escorted by a very intelligent and skilled Vendeuse, arrived.

On the Marquis's instructions she was helped into the dresses one after the other.

She then paraded in the Boudoir opening out of her bed-room.

The Marquis could see what she was wearing, and he described it to his Grandmother.

He was very firm in what he desired and the way he wanted her to look.

Once or twice, because the gown she was wearing seemed to her so beautiful, she wanted to argue with him.

When he shook his head she knew he was not thinking of the gown itself.

He was deciding whether it was the right frame for her looks, her hair, and her figure.

'Nothing really matters,' she told herself, 'as long as he admires me, and thinks I am beautiful.'

She was still afraid that she might wake up and find it had all been a dream.

She worried that the Marquis really admired women like her sister and she had just been deceived into thinking that he worshipped her.

Finally the dresses were chosen and the Special Licence, obtained from the Archbishop of Canterbury, arrived.

Ursa was told they were to be married the following morning and would then set off on their honeymoon.

"Where are we going?" she asked.

"That is a secret," he answered. "But I think, my Darling, you will find it very exciting."

"All I . . . want is to be . . . with you," Ursa said.

He gave a little laugh, then replied:

"Strangely enough, that is what I want too."

They looked at each other, and although the Marquis did not move, Ursa felt he was kissing her.

At the same time, she knew that his love for her, like hers for him, deepened every time they were alone together.

When she went to bed that night she prayed very hard that God would bless their marriage.

She prayed that she would never lose the Marquis and he would go on loving her as he did then.

'Please God, help me,' Ursa prayed. 'I know so little about his world and I cannot lose him.'

When finally she got into bed she felt as if the stars shining outside the window were telling her that her prayers had been heard.

The help she needed was there whenever she asked for it.

The Marquis had arranged that they were to be married at ten o'clock, which was not too early for his Grandmother.

He had chosen for Ursa a very beautiful white chiffon gown.

It clung to her body until it reached her waist.

Then it swung out into a very full skirt with frill upon frill trailing behind her.

It was simple, and yet it made her look translucent.

At the same time, she looked spiritual, as if she had just stepped down from the clouds.

The lace veil in her hair was very fine.

The Marquis gave her a diamond tiara which belonged to his Mother to wear over it.

"It was something I always hoped my wife would wear on my wedding day," the Marquis said. "And now, at last, my Darling, you shall have your engagement ring which I should have given you before."

The ring had a diamond shaped like a heart.

It had been fitted for the third finger of her left hand.

First he kissed her hand, and then the ring, before he put it on.

"I know that it will bring us both luck," he said, "and luck, as far as we are concerned, is something called love."

"It is beautiful," Ursa cried. "Thank you . . . thank . . . you."

Also to wear on her wedding morning was a diamond necklace and two small but very attractive diamond ear-rings.

When she was ready, the Marquis was waiting for her in the Boudoir.

When she came in he just stood and looked at her.

"That is just exactly how I wanted you to look," he said, "and how I shall think of you for the rest of our lives together."

She thought he would kiss her, but instead he handed her a bouquet which was made of white orchids.

He offered her his arm.

They went from the Boudoir, down the staircase, which avoided the servants in the hall.

It took them directly to the Chapel at the back of the Court.

It was a very beautiful Chapel, exquisitely painted.

The sun shone through a number of stained glass windows in a golden haze.

The candles were lit on the altar and there were flowers everywhere, all of them white.

They had been chosen, Ursa knew, because the Marquis thought they resembled her.

The Chaplain was waiting and the Dowager, Lady Brackley, was sitting in the front pew.

The organ which was hidden at the back of the Chapel was playing very softly.

But it was impossible to see who played it.

Because the marriage was secret, the Marquis had no Best-Man and the only witnesses were to be his Chaplain and his Grandmother.

The Chaplain read the Marriage Service with a deep sincerity.

It made Ursa feel that every word was a blessing from God Himself.

When they knelt again and the organ was still playing softly, she felt as if an Angel were singing overhead.

She and the Marquis were under the partition of Heaven.

When they rose from their knees without speaking, the Marquis took Ursa out of the Chapel and up the stairs down which they had come.

When they entered the Boudoir he took her to the communicating door to her bed-room.

He stopped and raised her hand to his lips.

First he kissed the finger on which was encircled his wedding ring, and then her hand.

"We leave as soon as you are ready, my Precious," he said very softly.

Then he left her.

The maids who had waited on her before she went downstairs helped her change into a travelling-gown with a cloak over it.

She had a very attractive bonnet which would not blow too much in the wind.

She knew they would be travelling in the Marquis's open Chaise with his fastest team to draw it, although she did not know yet where they were going.

When she went downstairs he was already changed and waiting for her.

Both he and his Grandmother had a glass of champagne in their hands.

"We are drinking your health, Dearest," the Dowager said. "And you too must drink to what I am sure will be the happiest day of your life."

"It is already," Ursa said. "I have never been so happy, and I think Guy is happy too."

"I will tell you how happy I am when we reach our destination," the Marquis replied.

Ursa still did not know what this was, but she knew she must not ask questions.

Instead, she drank a little champagne.

She kissed the Dowager "Good-bye."

"I shall miss you," Lady Brackley said. "And when you come home I hope you will ask me to stay here, unless you want to stay with me."

"We will do both," the Marquis said, "and we will write to you, Grandmama, and you must get

147

someone to write for you and tell us what you are doing."

"I will do that," the Dowager promised.

The Marquis kissed her and walked ahead, and as she kissed Ursa, she said:

"I cannot tell you, my Dear, how happy I am to have you in the family and to know that my precious grandson has found real happiness at last."

"Thank you, that is a lovely thing to say," Ursa said, "and I promise I will look after him."

"Do not forget, Dear," the Dowager begged.

Ursa said again:

"I will give him all my heart now and for ever."

She ran after the Marquis, and he helped her into the Chaise.

They set off with only a groom behind them on the back seat.

They drove very fast.

Only when they stopped for lunch at a large Posting-Inn did Ursa say a little tentatively:

"You know I am dying with curiosity to know where we are going."

"You have not guessed?" the Marquis asked.

She shook her head.

"Well, my yacht is in Dover harbour," he remarked.

She gave a little cry.

"We are going in a yacht? That is something I really enjoy. When Papa and I went to a great number of places in a ship, we always wished we had a yacht of our own."

"Well, that is what you have now," the Marquis answered. "I have changed its name to the 'Sea Nymph.' "

Ursa knew that was what her name meant in Greek.

She thought it was very touching that he should have renamed it.

The *"Sea Nymph"* was certainly a surprise.

It was much larger than Ursa had expected.

She learnt that the Marquis had it built originally so that he could try out on it the new ideas that he had for the Battleships.

"I will tell you all about it later," he said as they went aboard. "And now I am going to concentrate on one thing and one thing only, and that is my wife."

They had dinner in a house just outside Dover belonging to the Marquis.

It was what he sometimes used when he was going on a long journey which started early the following morning.

Alternatively, he used it when he came back to England and it was too late to return home.

It was only a small house but beautifully furnished.

The servants were delighted that their master was honouring them by his presence, and cooked a very special dinner.

The Dining-Room was decorated with flowers.

When they went aboard the *"Sea Nymph,"* Ursa found the master cabin, which filled the whole of the bow, was a bower of roses, lillies, orchids, and every other white flower obtainable.

As soon as they had come aboard, the yacht moved slowly out of harbour.

When they had gone a little way, the Marquis said:

"Now we will have a quiet night, without being disturbed, and tomorrow we set off for exciting new places, where I am hoping you have never been before."

"Tell me about them," Ursa begged.

He shook his head.

"I will tell you later," he said.

He went to the cabin next door, and Ursa undressed and got into bed.

It was a very large, very comfortable bed.

Lying in it, she could see the stars overhead.

When they anchored in the bay there was just the lap of the waves against the sides of the ship.

She did not have to wait long.

The door opened and the Marquis came in.

He stood for a moment, looking at her.

'No-one,' he thought, 'could look more beautiful with her fair hair falling over her shoulders.'

Then, as he got into bed and pulled her into his arms, he felt her quivering with excitement.

He knew for him this was the most exciting and thrilling moment of his life.

"I love you, my Precious, my adorable little wife," he said. "Now at last you belong to me and no-one can ever take you from me."

"I love . . . you," Ursa whispered.

"And I adore you," he said.

There was no need for words.

He kissed her until the rapture he evoked in her was rising higher and higher within her.

When his hands touched her body and drew her closer and closer to him, she felt as if he were carrying her up into the sky.

The stars were glittering in her breast.

The Marquis kissed her eyes, her cheeks, her lips, and in the softness of her neck.

It evoked a rapture Ursa had never known possible.

Then the stars in her breast turned strangely into little tongues of fire.

She felt it was impossible to feel such ecstasy and still be alive.

When the Marquis made her his, they were one person complete in each other now and for Eternity.

*   *   *

The Marquis spread the plans out on the table, saying:

"This is what we have to offer. It is up to you, because you speak Greek so much better than I do, to explain exactly what the effect will be on the ships we are using."

"I will do that," Ursa said, "and I hope he will be thrilled with what you have invented for him."

"What *we* have invented," the Marquis corrected Ursa. "You are part of this, my Precious, and a very big part."

"I think you are flattering me," Ursa said. "But I enjoy hearing you say so. But I am trying to understand the very complicated construction of a ship."

"I know that," the Marquis said, "and you have been absolutely brilliant so far. Orestes never stops telling me how wonderful you are until I feel jealous of his attention to you."

Ursa laughed.

She knew she had been very clever since they had arrived in Athens in making the Greeks appreciate even better than they had before the Marquis's inventions.

It was certainly bringing their Battleships up-to-date.

In fact, it put them in some ways ahead of all the other ships in the Mediterranean.

She thought it was the strangest honeymoon anyone could ever have.

The Marquis had taken her first to Africa because, he said, they were unknown there.

He wanted to speak to no-one and to look at no-one except herself.

It had been two weeks of such perfect happiness that Ursa could hardly bear to think they must leave.

Yet, as they moved slowly through the Mediterranean, the Marquis began to talk of his work for the first time.

Ursa found herself interested and thrilled in a very different way.

She understood exactly what he was asking her to do.

When they finally arrived in Athens, it was to find Mr. Orestes waiting for them.

She stepped into her part almost as if she had acted it a dozen times before.

The Greeks had certainly been very enthusiastic about everything that had been suggested to them.

Now it was time for them to move on, as they accepted the final plans.

"Where are we going?" Ursa asked.

There was a little pause, and she realised her husband was keeping something from her.

"What is it, what has happened?" she asked quickly.

"Nothing frightening, my precious one," he replied. "In fact, it is a very great compliment."

"What is?" Ursa asked.

"What I have here," the Marquis said.

He picked up from his desk an envelope, and Ursa saw it had an important-looking crest on it.

"Do you want to read it?" he asked. "Or shall I tell you?"

"You had better tell me," she said, "and soften the shock if there is one."

"It is not as bad as that," he said as he smiled.

He looked at her and then moved towards her.

"It is a long time since I kissed you," he said. "When you start talking to me like my partner and another man, I find myself forgetting for the moment the softness of your lips and how I like holding you in my arms."

He pulled her almost roughly against him.

Then he was kissing her possessively and passionately.

She knew the fire was burning once again in both of them.

"Darling, wait, we have work to do," Ursa managed to gasp.

"Work can wait; work is unimportant beside my need for you," the Marquis answered.

He took her from the cabin which they had made their study and into the one in which they slept.

He locked the door and lifted her on to the bed.

She did not protest because she loved him.

She knew that nothing was more important than the happiness they found in each other's arms.

He pulled off his coat and his tie and now he was kissing her.

It was impossible to think of anything but him and the ecstasy which was consuming them both.

"I love you," Ursa said.

"You are mine," the Marquis said, "mine completely. Tell me now if there is anything else of any importance except our love."

"You know there is nothing else," Ursa said. "I want you always to feel like this."

She knew as she spoke that they were flying up into the sky.

Now it was the sun that was waiting for them, the burning fiery sun which seemed to invade them both, and then there was only love, love which came from God.

*　　*　　*

It seemed a long time later before they went back to the cabin where their plans were lying open.

On top of them was the envelope they had been discussing.

"I had forgotten that this was what started it all," Ursa said with a smile.

The Marquis was looking at her in a rather strange way, and she asked:

"What is it, what have I done wrong?"

"I was just thinking how different you are from any other woman, and when I make love to you it seems as if it is something new I have never done

154

before," he answered. "It is the same, my Precious, with your adorable, active little brain. You never say what I expect you to say, it is always something which awakens new ideas and new inventions in me."

"Oh! Darling, I hope I can go on doing that," Ursa said. "Because working with you is nearly the most thrilling thing I have done in my life."

The Marquis's eyes twinkled.

"And what was the most thrilling?" he asked.

"You know without me telling you," she said.

"If you look at me like that," the Marquis said, "I will take you back next door and the subject of that letter that lies between us will never be raised."

Ursa laughed.

"Tell me now and get it over with. Is it something that is going to frighten me?"

"I hope not," the Marquis replied.

He opened the letter and said:

"As it is in French, and your French is as good if not better than mine, you had better read it."

Although she was a little apprehensive, Ursa took it from him.

As she held it in her hand she saw it was from the French Ministry and concerned the Navy.

It did not take her long to read it, and it was extremely complimentary.

The French Chargé d'Affaires said he had heard of the tremendous work and innovations the Marquis had made on the Greek Navy.

He had the pleasure of asking him if at his own convenience he would visit Marseille and discuss improvements on the French fleet.

Ursa read through it, and then she said:

"Is it possible that you have become so important that everyone is going to want you? And you will have to make them wait in a queue before you receive them like a Sultan or a King."

The Marquis laughed.

"It sounds very impressive. But at the same time, my Darling, it is a compliment and I suppose it is something we should accept."

"They say there is no hurry," Ursa said.

"Yes, I read that," he answered. "But I cannot think of any reasons why we should wait. Perhaps the Italians, the Germans, and even the Scandinavians may be requiring our services."

"Why not?" Ursa said. "At the same time, I have another suggestion to make, which you may not like."

The Marquis looked at her.

"Why should you say that?"

She rose from the table where she had been sitting while she read the letter from France.

She walked to the porthole.

Outside, the sun was shining and the sea was blue of the Madonna's Robes.

The Islands in the distance were very beautiful.

Then the Marquis was behind her and he said:

"What is worrying you, and what are you trying to tell me?"

For a moment Ursa did not move, and then she turned quickly and hid her face against his neck.

His arms went round her.

"What is it, my Precious?"

"I just think it . . . would be . . . nice if we . . . went home."

For a moment the Marquis was still, and then he said:

"Any particular reason?"

"I think . . . you have . . . guessed what . . . it is," Ursa said very softly.

His arms tightened.

"It is true, then, you are quite sure?"

"Our first child," she said in a voice he could hardly hear, "will be born in about six months' time, and I want to be at home."

"So do I," the Marquis said.

He pulled her closer still as he said:

"Are you quite certain?"

"I saw a Doctor this morning, when you were with Mr. Orestes. He congratulated me on looking and feeling so well, and as far as he was concerned, everything was perfect."

The Marquis's lips were close to hers.

"My Darling, my Precious," he said, "you know what this means to me."

"And to me," she said. "And you did want a large family?"

"The larger the better," he said. "We have got to fill the Court and a great number of other houses before we have finished."

Ursa laughed.

"Now you are going too fast, but I hope the first baby is just like you and just as wonderful."

"You are not to love him more than you love me," the Marquis said. "But I think, my Darling, we shall be very proud of him and if he has our brains, then he will be a very helpful addition to the staff."

Ursa laughed.

"You are still going too fast," she said. "Firstly, I want him to be English and to love the horses and all the things you have at Charnwood. It does seem quite a while since we have been at home."

"And that is where we are going," the Marquis said. "The French can wait, but we will call as we pass Marseille and assure them that they have their rightful place in the queue."

Ursa laughed.

"Now you are being very autocratic."

"That is what I intend to be as Father of my family," the Marquis said.

He pulled her a little closer.

"I love you, I love you," he said, "and as you say, our first son will be a very important person to us both and I hope eventually to the world."

"Just like you are, my Darling," Ursa murmured.

"If I am important, it is because that is what you are making me," the Marquis said. "But you are quite right, we must not forget our own country and our own people, the people you told me about a long time ago who were important to me because they worked on my land and looked to me to solve their problems and their troubles and preserve their happiness."

"And that is what you have been doing," Ursa said. "But at the same time, I think they should see you and talk to you, and who knows, we might find a mass of new ideas which will be as useful to the countryside as the ships are to the sea."

"That is exactly what we shall do," the Marquis agreed. "But, my Darling, I have not yet told you how thrilled I am by your news and how much it means to me and how you, my Nymph of the Sea, are everything in my life. In fact, the beginning of it and the end, and I can do nothing without you."

"That is what I want you to think even though it is not quite true," Ursa said. "But it is true to tell you, Guy, that every day I love you more than I loved you yesterday and now, because this is a very special day, I love you with all my heart and soul."

"I also want your brain and—your beautiful body," the Marquis added.

Then as he was kissing her, there was no need to say any more.

ABOUT THE AUTHOR

Barbara Cartland, the world's most famous romantic novelist, who is also an historian, playwright, lecturer, political speaker and television personality, has now written 608 books and sold over six hundred and twenty million copies all over the world.

She has also had many historical works published and has written four autobiographies as well as the biographies of her mother and that of her brother, Ronald Cartland, who was the first Member of Parliament to be killed in the last war. This book has a preface by Sir Winston Churchill and has just been republished with an introduction by Sir Arthur Bryant.

Love at the Helm, a novel written with the help and inspiration of the late Earl Mountbatten of Burma, Great Uncle of His Royal Highness, The Prince of Wales, is being sold for the Mountbatten Memorial Trust.

She has broken the world record for the last twenty years by writing an average of twenty-three books a year. In the *Guinness Book of World Records* she is listed as the world's top-selling author.

Miss Cartland in 1987 sang an Album of Love Songs with the Royal Philharmonic Orchestra.

In private life Barbara Cartland, who is a Dame of the Order of St. John of Jerusalem and Chairman of the St. John Council in Hertfordshire, has fought for better conditions and salaries for Midwives and Nurses.

She championed the cause for the Elderly in 1956, invoking a Government Enquiry into the "Housing Condition of Old People."

In 1962 she had the Law of England changed so that Local Authorities had to provide camps for their own Gypsies. This has meant that since then thousands and thousands of Gypsy children have been able to go to School, which they had never been able to do in the past, as their caravans were moved every twenty-four hours by the Police.

There are now fifteen camps in Hertfordshire and Barbara Cartland has her own Romany Gypsy Camp called "Barbaraville" by the Gypsies.

Her designs "Decorating with Love" are being sold all over the U.S.A. and the National Home Fashions League made her, in 1981, "Woman of Achievement."

She is unique in that she was one and two in the Dalton list of Best Sellers, and one week had four books in the top twenty.

Barbara Cartland's book *Getting Older, Growing Younger* has been published in Great Britain and the U.S.A. and her fifth cookery book, *The Romance of Food*, is now being used by the House of Commons.

In 1984 she received at Kennedy Airport America's Bishop Wright Air Industry Award for her contribution to the development of aviation. In 1931 she and two R.A.F. Officers thought of, and carried, the first aeroplane-towed glider airmail.

During the War she was Chief Lady Welfare Officer in Bedfordshire, looking after 20,000 Servicemen and women. She thought of having a pool of Wedding Dresses at the War Office so a Service Bride could hire a gown for the day.

She bought 1,000 gowns without coupons for the A.T.S., the W.A.A.F.'s and the W.R.E.N.S. In 1945 Barbara Cartland received the Certificate of Merit from Eastern Command.

In 1964 Barbara Cartland founded the National Association for Health of which she is the President, as a front for all the Health Stores and for any product made as alternative medicine.

This is now a £65 million turnover a year, with one-third going in export.

In January 1968 she received *La Médeille de Vermeil de la Ville de Paris*. This is the highest award to be given in France by the City of Paris. She has sold 30 million books in France.

In March 1988 Barbara Cartland was asked by the Indian Government to open their Health Resort outside Delhi. This is almost the largest Health Resort in the world.

Barbara Cartland was received with great enthusiasm by her fans, who feted her at a reception in the City, and she received the gift of an embossed plate from the Government.

Barbara Cartland was made a Dame of the Order of the British Empire in the 1991 New Year's Honours List by Her Majesty, The Queen, for her contribution to Literature and also for her years of work for the community.

Dame Barbara has now written 608 books, the greatest number by a British author, passing the 564 books written by John Creasey.

AWARDS

1945   Received Certificate of Merit, Eastern Command, for being Welfare Officer to 5,000 troops in Bedfordshire.

1953   Made a Commander of the Order of St. John of Jerusalem. Invested by H.R.H. The Duke of Gloucester at Buckingham Palace.

1972   Invested as Dame of Grace of the Order of St. John in London by The Lord Prior, Lord Cacia.

1981   Received "Achiever of the Year" from the National Home Furnishing Association in Colorado Springs, U.S.A., for her designs for wallpaper and fabrics.

1984   Received Bishop Wright Air Industry Award at Kennedy Airport, for inventing the aeroplane-towed Glider.

1988   Received from Monsieur Chirac, The Prime Minister, The Gold Medal of the City of Paris, at the Hotel de la Ville, Paris, for selling 25 million books and giving a lot of employment.

1991   Invested as Dame of the Order of The British Empire, by H.M. The Queen at Buckingham Palace for her contribution to Literature.